Edward C. Millard, Lucy E. Guinness

**South America - the Neglected Continent**

being an account of the mission tour of G. C. Grubb, and party, in 1893

Edward C. Millard, Lucy E. Guinness

**South America - the Neglected Continent**
*being an account of the mission tour of G. C. Grubb, and party, in 1893*

ISBN/EAN: 9783337221225

Printed in Europe, USA, Canada, Australia, Japan

Cover: Foto ©Andreas Hilbeck / pixelio.de

More available books at **www.hansebooks.com**

# South America

# The Neglected Continent

BEING AN ACCOUNT OF THE MISSION TOUR OF THE REV. G. C. GRUBB, M.A., AND
PARTY, IN 1893, WITH A HISTORICAL SKETCH AND SUMMARY OF
MISSIONARY ENTERPRISE IN THESE VAST REGIONS

BY

## E. C. MILLARD

AND

## LUCY E. GUINNESS

FLEMING H. REVELL COMPANY
NEW YORK     CHICAGO     TORONTO
*Publishers of Evangelical Literature*

# PREFACE.

BELOVED BROTHER OR SISTER IN OUR LORD JESUS CHRIST,—

May I ask you before reading this little book to spend one minute in prayer. Ask the God of all grace to bring the desires of your heart and the determination of your will into harmony with His purposes of grace towards South America. Our chief object in publishing this volume is to cause a stream of prayer to flow forth from the hearts of Christians—that they may pray "everywhere, lifting up holy hands without wrath and doubting."

God has revealed wondrous purposes with regard to the future blessing of Israel; but He adds, "I will for this be *enquired* of by the house of Israel, to do it for them." God has also purposes of grace towards the nations of the whole earth; but He adds, "*Ask* of Me, and I shall give thee the nations for thine inheritance, and the uttermost parts of the earth for thy possession."

May God pour on each member of the one body the spirit of grace and of supplication, that he may be able to join with the prayers of Christ for South America.

For nearly four hundred years Romanism of the most corrupt type

5

has spread its blighting influence over this vast continent. The true and unfailing harvest of Romanism,—namely, indifference, sensuality, infidelity, and anarchy,—is being plentifully reaped. Praise be to God there are sure signs that the Spirit of God is moving over this dark waste of waters, and soon "Let there be light" will sound from north to south, from east to west.

That this little book may help to bruise Satan under our feet shortly and hasten the coming of earth's rightful King, is the prayer of

Yours in that Blessed Hope,

*Jan. 1st,* 1894. GEORGE C. GRUBB.

# CONTENTS.

## PART I.—THE MISSION TOUR.

## PART II.—HISTORICAL SURVEY AND SUMMARY.

*C*OMMUNICATIONS *from*
     *Friends volunteering for Service or desirous of assisting, by gift or in any other way, in **Mission Work in South** America, may be sent to*

### IN ENGLAND.

Mr. G. E. JACKSON, Missionary Training Home, 10, Drayton Park, London, N.

Mr. H. MAXWELL WRIGHT, c o E. Marlborough & Co., 51, Old Bailey, London, E.C.

Dr. H. GRATTAN GUINNESS, The East London Institute for Home and Foreign Missions, Harley House, Bow, London, E.

### IN AUSTRALASIA.

Dr. and Mrs. WARREN, Training Home, Exeter, South Melbourne, Victoria.

— -

*\*\* Any profits accruing from sale of this book will be devoted to Missionary Work in South America.*

# The Neglected Continent.

## PART I.

### Mission Tour of Rev. G. C. Grubb, M.A., and Party.

E. C. MILLARD.

# THE NEGLECTED CONTINENT.

## CHAPTER I.

"Where are the reapers?
Oh, who will come
And share the joy of the harvest-home?
Oh, who will help us
To gather in
The sheaves of good from the fields of sin?"

"*Go ye into* ALL THE WORLD, *and preach the gospel to* EVERY CREATURE."

HAVING lately returned from a short visit to some of the English Communities in Argentina, Uruguay, and Brazil, our hearts are stirred beyond measure with the sense of the tremendous responsibility which falls upon every professing follower of the LORD JESUS CHRIST with regard to the thirty-seven million souls of South America.

The conviction deepens that some definite steps should be taken; and with this object in view, we feel it to be necessary for information to be spread far and wide as to the existing need and the opportunities for work. To this we add a few words of testimony to the power of GOD, exercised over

QUARTERMASTER.

PHOTOGRAPH OF THE PARTY, BY W. BARNETT, ESQ.

the' hearts of those with whom we were brought into contact during the one hundred and twenty-eight days of our tour.

The invitation originally came from a single individual, W. Barnett Esq., of Rosario de Santa Fé, in the Argentine Republic, whose attention had been drawn to Mr. Grubb's mission through reading an account of a tour in other places recorded in our previous book, *What God hath Wrought*,[1] and to whom we are indebted for the annexed block from a photograph of the party taken on his garden steps. As a member of the Committee of the South American Missionary Society, Mr. Barnett was instrumental in getting us a written welcome from the Bishop of the Falkland Islands, who was heartily supported in the matter by the ministers of other Churches.

The promoters of the Keswick Convention contributed the sum of £300 from the Missionary fund, to assist in carrying out the work; the

[1] *What God hath Wrought.* E. Marlborough & Co., 51, Old Bailey, London.

balance of expenditure being met by unsolicited donations from Christian friends in those places where Missions were subsequently conducted. The Committee of the South American Missionary Society showed warm sympathy in the effort, and arranged a special Farewell Service, in St. Dunstan's Church, on Wednesday morning, the 19th of April, 1893. In the afternoon, at the invitation of the Rev. C. A. Fox, a prayer meeting was held at Eaton Chapel,

SOME OF THE 1ST-CLASS PASSENGERS.

when the mission about to be undertaken was committed definitely into the hands of the LORD—"Our weakness" *v.* 'GOD's strength," being the keynote of all that was then said. Next day we sailed from Southampton Docks for South America.

Most of the passengers on board with us were young men, going out to follow their professions in different parts of the Continent, viz., Pernambuco, Bahia, Rio de Janeiro, Buenos Ayres, and Valparaiso.

Our first thought, therefore, was, that we should ask the LORD to work by His Spirit in the hearts of these young men; for unconverted traders are too frequently the cause of much hindrance in the Mission field. It is a matter of the most vital importance that all classes of men, in whatever calling, should be possessed by the power of GOD, to enable them to be witnesses unto Him in the countries where they go as representatives of a Christian land, and who are consequently looked upon as Christians by the natives amongst whom they live. An English-speaking Chinaman in Foochow once made this remark: "I do not understand you Christians, because one-half of you come here to *teach* us to do what is *right*, and the other half *pay* us to do what is *wrong*."

As opportunities offered we conversed with one and another on board, and praise the LORD, several were brought face to face with the truth, and more than one professed to have received definite blessing from GOD. Some opposition came from a quarter where one would least have expected it. How deeply it is to be regretted that clergy, ministers, and missionaries are sometimes sent out, who are not only wholly unfit to do spiritual work, but who spend their leisure time reading *Yellow Backs*, and sneer at the sight of a Bible read in open day.

The right sort of Missionaries—men who believe in conversion, who have themselves been converted, and who know it—to say nothing of the necessity of being also "endued with power from on high"—are badly wanted for South America, so that they may be witnesses . . . in these uttermost parts of the earth.

It is heart-breaking to see unconverted religious professors landing in a heathen land; but such is too often the case.

Different societies at times bemoan the fact that there is a balance on the wrong side at the end of their financial year, and special efforts are made to replenish their coffers; but the reason that the dollars are scarce, may be, and, I fear, often is, because GOD's stewards are withheld from contributing to the cause on account of want of confidence in some of those sent out as "preachers of the Gospel."

Many a young business man is blamed for living an ungodly life in a heathen city; but it is not always wholly to be wondered at, when one meets clergy of the Church of England who do not believe in conversion, and Nonconformist ministers who doubt the authenticity of the Scriptures; while matters are made still worse by the fact that these very young men on their outward journey are hindered rather than helped by the example of some shepherds of GOD's flock.

Life on board ship provides one of the best testing times for any Missionary, and ample opportunity is then and there offered for service. Talk about the romance of preaching to the heathen! Why, there are often absolute heathen to be found all around one. To give one or two instances :—

One afternoon Mr. Grubb and I were standing by the steerage companion ladder, when an old man of the ship's company, with his bucket and washer, passed by, and said to Mr. Grubb, "You haven't been down our end yet, sir!"

"No," said Mr. Grubb. "We left you alone for the first day or two. Are there any Christians among the sailors and firemen?"

He only shook his head!

"Have *you* trusted the LORD for yourself?"

"Oh, yes," said he; "this last sixty-two years, and I have been aboard this vessel twenty years."

Not feeling very sure but that his trust in the LORD was merely a sailor's belief in "th' Almighty above us," I asked him if he thought he would be ready to stand before GOD at the judgment day.

"Oh, yes," said he.

"But what reason have you for thinking that your soul will be safe at that day?"

"Because, sir, I never troubles myself about nothing. I never looks a 'ead; I does my work, and looks after my 'ome, and that's all as I can see that's wanted!"

"How old are you?" said I.

"Sixty-two, sir."

We explained the way of salvation just as we would to a heathen, and it all seemed as new to him that JESUS died to save him, as if he had never heard it before.

There was also a young fellow of twenty-four years of age, travelling second class, who was converted just before leaving England, and who began to read his Bible for the first time. One morning he came up to Mr.

A NATIVE SWIMMING RACE, ST. VINCENT, CAPE VERDE ISLANDS.

Grubb, while he was sitting on deck, and said, in a simple, childlike way, " I can't find the story where Cain killed his brother, and I've looked all through the New Testament for it." We discovered that he had been brought up in the Romish Church, and therefore knew nothing of the Scriptures.

A young woman, who tried to pass herself off as a Christian, seemed glad for us to converse with her, but complained that in her sphere of life it was impossible to be a real Christian. As the conversation led on to the subject of believing, and then taking up the Cross of testimony to follow JESUS, even if it meant persecution from one's own relatives and friends, I quoted John i. 11, how that JESUS came unto His own people, and "His own received Him not." She turned to me, and said, "Well, then, from what you say, JESUS was a *Jew*; but I always thought He was a Catholic."

A lady's maid became convicted through overhearing some conversation, and joining in, said with a sigh, "I hope I'll live a long life, and do some good things before I die, so that I shall get to heaven; for although I've tried many times, I've never done any good deeds yet, and I've done plenty of wickedness."

Such facts speak for themselves, and show the necessity of Missionaries being ready to witness anywhere, and not waiting till they reach some heathen land; like the young lady who, when asked if she would join in a meeting among the sailors, replied, "My work does not begin till I get to ———," naming the Mission Station where she was to work among heathen women.

The sailors and firemen were the most encouraging to deal with, on three or four occasions asking us of their own accord to "Come down and have a sing." They seemed to enjoy hearing the Bible read aloud, and explained as one went along, better than anything. At one meeting, Mr. Grubb had a most attentive crowd round him, down in the forecastle, when he went through the first four chapters of the Gospel of John.

Before the voyage was over, many were blessed, and it was a decided change to hear Sankey's Hymns sounding up through the grating above the stoke-hole; for many of the men, by the power of GOD, had a new song put into their mouths, and swearing was turned into singing. Several having expressed a wish for a Bible, were asked to put down their names, so as to

find out how many were wanted, and a list of forty-one was handed in.
Glory be to GOD!

Quarantine regulations kept us four days at anchor in the River Plate—
a delay which gave us further opportunities of dealing with the souls on
board, and enabled us to have special prayer together for the Missions about
to be conducted. We were here privileged to see one of those magnificent
southern sunsets for which this part of the
country is so famed, any attempt at verbal
description of which seems utterly feeble.
At the close of an afternoon of writing in
the saloon, we came up on deck, and stood
at the stern of the ship. A solemn silence
came over us all as we were attracted by the
wonderful glory. The sky was broken with
drifting clouds, and though the sun itself
was not visible, it threw a widespread glow
of fiery red on the horizon, making the water
look a dark neutral tint, while five-and-
thirty to forty steamers and sailing vessels
lay still and heavy upon it, as the tide flowed
against their bows.

LARGE BOAT.

The lines of fleecy clouds stretching across
the sky above the fiery glow were rich with
liquid gold, and the glare was so strong, even upon these lofty steamers, that
they were quite dazzling to behold.

Just as we were about to break the felt silence by remarking that the
picture was past improvement, a barque in full sail, coming noiselessly up
behind us, quietly passed into the scene. Presently the sailors went aloft,
and reefed the tops'ls ; a few moments more, and they further reduced
the canvas, and before she had coursed her way up the river another hundred

yards, the masts were undressed, the anchor let go, and she too rode upon the bosom of the water, and seemingly passed off to sleep. The light changed, the colours faded, darkness crept slowly over us, and the clouds, which in themselves were nothing, except that they had a capacity for reflecting the glory of the sun soon hung in ponderous black masses—and it was night.

# CHAPTER II.

EARLY MORNING, RIVER DE LA PLATA.

N the morning of the 22nd of May the delay was at an end, and we found ourselves alongside of the docks at Ensenada. We were met by the clergy and ministers of the different Churches, the secretary of the Y.M.C.A., Mr. Barnett, and other Christian friends, who, having prayed long and earnestly, wished to give us a welcome, and to encourage us to believe in the power of GOD.

Before we had put a foot on shore, however, the devil began to show his disapproval of a renewed attack on his kingdom, for Mr. Grubb received what might have been a fatal blow. As he stepped across the deck to say goodbye to the captain, a large iron block, many pounds in weight, fell from the rigging with tremendous force upon his head. For a moment the sailors held their breath, expecting that his head had been cut open; but, praise GOD, there was only a slight graze.

One of the quarter-masters remarked that he could not make out how he had escaped, to which he replied with a smile, "There must have been an

PLAZA VICTORIA BUENOS AYRES.

angel about, or I might have been badly hurt." "He shall give His angels charge over thee, lest at any time    . ."

A journey of between twenty and thirty miles by rail from Ensenada brought us to the city of Buenos Ayres: where, passing from the station to

the Plaza Victoria, we separated in different directions, each escorted by
kind friends, who warmly invited us to their homes.

The streets of this busy and populous Spanish city struck us as being
very dirty, and we were informed that, unless favoured by heavy showers, the
roads remain unwashed, and the citizens are expected to be satisfied with
"skating" along over greasy flags, while the outlying districts indulge in
beautiful mud, the roads in rainy seasons being frequently several inches
under water. The city is built in squares, and the tram service, running at
right angles, is reputed to be the most complete in the world. The horses,
however, suffer fearfully from the bad state of the roads, and the attention of
the newly-arrived foreigner is arrested by the dinning noise of the drivers'
"penny trumpets," which
the law compels them to
blow on approaching every
crossing at the corners of
the squares.

Milk is supplied to the
inhabitants either by the
cows being led to the front
door and milked before
one's eyes, or from the cans
of the léchéros, who ride
many miles to the town
from the estancias. Churns
for making butter are rarely
used, as the jog-trot of the
horses sufficiently shakes
the milk, and so answers
the same purpose. Should
there not be a large enough

TIPO DE LECHEROS.

supply of butter when the man first arrives, he will say, " Not quite ready yet ; but I will ride round the town, and call again," and by the time he returns the quantity will have largely increased.

Roman Catholic chapels, with their attendant priests and nuns, abound ; while both black and white beggars stand asking an alms in the porches of these idolatrous temples.

The Republic, which seems to be in an everlasting state of revolution, is by no means confident in the Government officials. Soldiers are frequently called out to settle some party squabble, and owing to want of proper management, the bullets have been known to be lodged in the heads of the unfortunate people to whose assistance the military had been sent.

POVERTY AND FINANCE.

Miniature police, who seem to be the smallest men in the country, are stationed with a sword and whistle at the corner of every square, and their authority is enforced, if necessary, by a show of their weapon. But "Red Tape" is very prominent in this department of the Government. On one occasion a man was run over by a tram, his leg being almost severed from his body. Some philanthropic Englishmen rushed to his assistance ; but the police drew swords, and stood over him till authority should be given from the chief constable to have the man removed to the hospital. Meanwhile the poor victim bled to death !

On another occasion a young Spaniard, in a restaurant, accidentally swallowed a chicken-bone, which stuck in his throat. Running into the street, he signed to a man to thump him on the back ; but as the man was about to comply with the request, the important police arrived on the spot, and with drawn swords stood by, allowing the poor fellow to choke to death in the gutter !

Gambling seems to be one of the chief national vices, and many a young Englishman has been led on to desperation through frequenting the saloons set apart for this purpose.

"Why do not the authorities put a stop to it?" is the question often asked when murder and suicide have been the result of a midnight loss. Because the Government officials themselves are again and again to be found in these dens: and history relates that some years ago one of the presidents of the Republic, having staked his last dollar, and seeing he was about to lose, cried, "If I lose now, I will shut up this place." Of course the proprietors took care that the real winner was bribed to waive his position, and the house, which was one of the most important of its class, was allowed to continue with its devilish excitement and maddening fascination.

Immorality, too, is looked upon as a necessity; so that eventually it becomes a proverb that "To do wrong is to do right."

The thunder-clap threats of purgatorial torture brought down upon the heads of priest-ridden people (in some parts of Ireland, for instance) have been known to put a certain moral restraint upon individuals through fear; but the laxity of even this teaching, and the openly drunken and sensual lives of some of the priests in South America, has only tended to encourage both men and women to dash along in unhindered folly. Well may the cry be uttered from the heart of the REDEEMER: "How shall I pardon thee for this? Thy children have forsaken Me, and sworn by them that are no gods. When I had fed them to the full, they then committed adultery, and assembled themselves by troops in harlots' houses. They were as fed horses in the morning: every one neighed after his neighbour's wife. Shall I not visit for these things? saith the Lord: and shall not My soul be avenged on such a nation as this?" (Jer. v. 7-9).

Would to GOD that such open wickedness might be limited to even some little extent; but, sad to say, not a few of England's brightest sons and purest daughters have been allured into these heart-breaking devilries, and—must we say it?—the donning of ecclesiastical robes and the laying on of a Bishop's hands does not deliver a man from *feu d'enfer*.

There are, however, GOD's faithful witnesses in this grievous land, and by some of these a hearty welcome was offered to us, as, with about thirty others, we met for our opening meeting in the upper room of the Y.M.C.A.

With the very first words of Mr. Grubb's message our faith began to rise: "Power belongeth unto GOD." "For they gat not the land in possession by their own sword, neither did their own arm save them; but *Thy* right hand, and *Thine* arm, and the light of *Thy* countenance" (Ps. xliv. 3–8). "How does GOD choose to work? Through the instrumentality of His believing people." JESUS said to His disciples, "I tell you the truth. It is expedient for you that I go away: for

CHURCH OF THE HOLY TRINITY, LOMAS DE ZAMORA.

if I go not away, the COMFORTER will not come unto you ; but if I depart, I will send Him *unto you.* And when He is come (unto you), He will convict the world of sin, and of righteousness, and of judgment."

The power of GOD was upon the meeting, and many earnest petitions were sent up to the throne of grace, that the COMFORTER might have free entrance into the hearts of His people, and that as the result conviction might be upon those living in rebellion against the LORD.

At the invitation of the Rev. Canon Pinchard, the first Mission was conducted in the Church of the Holy Trinity, in Lomas de Zamora.

The numbers who attended this suburban church were not large, and although there were some distinct cases of blessing among them, and many of the lambs of GOD's flock sought and found the GOOD SHEPHERD, there seemed to be little more than mere conviction, except in the cases of the more earnest Christians, who were much refreshed by the sound of the Gospel every time they came.

Feeling that there was a block in the way of GOD's Chariot of Salvation, we met, with several of the promoters of the Mission, on the Saturday after-noon in the secretary's office of the Y.M.C.A. In that room were gathered together those who had for years past mingled tears with their prayers, having cried with strong agony, and who felt that now the wave of the expected revival was not far distant. There were others who, though brothers in CHRIST, had been somewhat wide apart through devil-created differences, which now were all swept away ; and as the Spirit of love and prayer was poured upon us, and the victory won by faith, we rejoiced with great joy, so that the two hours passed with astonishing rapidity. Hearts were united in the bond of peace, and there was a unity of desire that we should work together for the strengthening of believers and the conversion of souls.

" Little children, love one another."

THE Sunday Edition of the daily paper at Buenos Ayres is well patronised, and the fact that there is a Sabbath of rest is taken advantage of for "doing one's pleasure on GOD's holy day" (Isa. lviii. 13). The paper is, of course, the great medium for announcements, both secular and religious, and one could not help being attracted to the column with the heading, "Events for Sunday," by seeing the three items, "Football," "Polo," "Grubb."

THE LECTURE HALL, CALLE CORRIENTES.

The Sunday Observance question has been much fought over in times past, and we saw in *The Review of the River Plate* the following remarks with reference to Mr. Grubb's proposed visit :—

A special Evangelical mission is shortly expected to land upon these shores. Its advent will, we are afraid, resuscitate the vexed question of Sunday observance, and we shall probably have again to go through the disagreeable experience of a reiteration of threats of Eternal damnation hurled at the devoted heads of those who take their recreation upon the sabbath.

When asked in what way we would deal with this "vexed question," we were led to give this one answer : " If a young man becomes really converted, delivered from the love of the world, and filled with the HOLY GHOST, he will not want to play polo on Sunday."

A young fellow said to me one day while walking to a service, " If I become a real Christian, can I go to the theatre if I like ? "

" Certainly," said I, " if you like ! "

" But," said he, " I thought all of you looked upon these things as wrong and you say you never go."

" I can go to the theatre if I like," I replied.

" Why don't you go, then ? " said he, rather puzzled.

" Because *I don't like*," said I, " for the LORD has changed my taste for all these things, and it would be no pleasure to me to frequent a theatre. But I find great delight in serving the LORD, and that is a salvation worth having. Anything short of this shows that there is something wrong in our spiritual condition, for we read, ' Love not the world, neither the things that are in the world. If any man love the world, the love of the FATHER is not in him. For all that is in the world, the lust of the flesh, the lust of the eyes, and the pride of life, is not of the FATHER, but is of the world. And the world passeth away, and the lust thereof : but he that doeth the will of GOD abideth for ever ' " (1 John ii. 15-17).

After much prayer as to the next step to take, it was brought home to us very strongly that the LORD would have us meet daily with the Christians of Buenos Ayres, and consider the subject of the deepening of spiritual life, before attempting any evangelistic effort for the unconverted.

The offer of the Lecture Hall at the back of the American Methodist Episcopal Church having been made by the pastor, the Rev. W. P. McLaughlin, D.D., we held three meetings each day for a week. The first three days were times of deep conviction, when Christians of all denominations met together, and were brought face to face with truths that had been long hidden from their view. Thursday and Friday were days of surrender, and many who had hitherto been living defeated lives claimed deliverance from the traitor spirit, and opening their hearts to "the KING OF GLORY," welcomed Him in, who is able to keep us, and lead us onward, upward, in the life of perpetual victory.

Believers' unbelief having been removed, and faith in GOD strengthened, we felt that the time had come for an invitation to those who knew not GOD.

THE AMERICAN METHODIST EPISCOPAL CHURCH.

Several special efforts were made by different resident Christians to persuade their friends to attend the services. One lady obtained permission from the manager of the chief English restaurant, and delivered cards of invitation to the gentlemen as they sat at their lunch, with the result that a convicted opponent put an angry article in the daily paper. Another gentleman who was present, finding the article not altogether true on some points, and feeling that a lady should not be thus publicly insulted, sent a stinging reply. He also came to the Mission, and was himself converted.

The attendance increased, and on one drenching night (several having to wade up to their knees to reach their homes afterwards) there were present no less than 110 men and 35 women.

The SPIRIT OF GOD worked mightily, and in addition to many who received blessing, fourteen young men professed CHRIST as their Saviour, and several backsliders were restored. Some of the Christian young men were so convicted of their lukewarm Christianity that they completely broke down, and one of them told me that he must take the blame to himself that none of the fellows in his office had been saved ; for, said he, " My Christianity has been enough to make any one say they would have nothing to do with it."

One night, after the meeting had concluded and several young men were on their knees seeking deliverance from besetting sins, one, who had been a professing Christian for ten years, came up to me and said, with great emotion, " Can I have a few words with you?" Retiring to an adjoining room, he looked the picture of misery, and said, " Brother, you must excuse me if I break right up to-night, for the SPIRIT OF GOD has been convincing me that my past Christian life has been worse than useless." The words were hardly uttered when he did in very truth "break up," and the foundations of his deep grief poured forth uncontrollable groans and weeping. Oh ! how he emptied out his whole heart to the SAVIOUR, and what a volume of pleading for deliverance reached the ever-open ear of the sheep-seeking Shepherd! After a while he prayed, —

" Oh, my God, I have surrounded myself with a fog and mist of my own creation. I have brought all this darkness upon myself, and I can only say that it would have been better if I had never been born, rather than to have brought this shame to Thy name ; but if Thou canst do anything, if the ray of Thy love can pierce through my darkness, then come, oh come, and penetrate my soul, cleanse my heart, and take me now."

Silence, sacred silence, followed. The SAVIOUR'S voice was heard, and the ray of His restoring love burst in upon him, and resting on the promises of GOD, his mourning was turned into praising, in that he was pardoned and cleansed, and could go forth in the power of the HOLY GHOST to serve under His banner.

Later on I found eight young men in Mr. Grubb's bedroom, all down on their knees, calling upon GOD. Some of them had been the objects of much prayer—two in particular the sons of a devoted mother, whose cries from the old home had reached the throne of GOD. The hand of power was stretched forth, and salvation wrought in the hearts and lives of her beloved boys.

Another, a married man, terribly hardened by continual failure in the attempt to "keep" himself (though a prominent Christian before leaving home for South America), was attracted to these meetings by a fellow-clerk in his office, whom the LORD had blessed at the Mission. He came again and again, till at last the truth of 1 John i. 9 came home to him, and laying aside his sin by faith, he dared to believe that the LORD would deliver him from the very desire of drink. He had described his case as that of being bound down with iron chains, but he rejoiced greatly in the promise in Isaiah xlv. 2: "I will go before thee, and break in pieces the gates of brass, and cut in sunder the bars of iron." He was afterwards able to testify, "He *hath* broken the gates of brass, and cut the bars of iron in sunder" (Ps. cvii. 16).

ORNAMENTAL ROCKERY, BUENOS AYRES.

One of the leading Christians brought in to an evening service two men who were to some extent the worse for liquor. During the meeting they were both broken down, and before eleven o'clock that night went away rejoicing in the LORD as their SAVIOUR. Although for a time they did run well, Satan has hindered them, and we hear that they have gone sadly back. Will every one who reads this pray for them? for the LORD has work for them yet. "Be not faithless, but believing."

The Sunday services were numerous, for the pulpits of the Church of England, Scotch Episcopal,[1] and American Methodist were all thrown open, while the Sunday-schools were visited, the members of the Y.W.C.A. and Y.M.C.A. addressed at their afternoon Bible Classes, and a special meeting held among the sailors at the Boca Mission Room, under the charge of Mr. Walker, of the South American Missionary Society. Services in Spanish, under the superintendence of Dr. Thompson and Dr. Drees, of the American Church, were densely crowded and much blessed. On several occasions Mr. Grubb spoke by interpretation. This Spanish portion of the work is most interesting, but is very much *crippled by the lack of workers.* Men and women are wanted to teach, preach, and witness to hungry souls by the power of the HOLY GHOST. Crowded audiences are easily secured; but where are the messengers to reach them?

The Young Men's Christian Association has Mr. Barnett as president, and is conducted on spiritual lines, and is not in debt. We are constantly hearing that since the Mission new members are being added every week, and much blessing is rolling along. The editor of their organ, *The Gleaner*, is much interested in the work among the Spanish people, and conducts open-air meetings for them, and also has a Sunday-school for Spanish children. Mr. Holder, the secretary, told us that the Spanish people are most willing to be taught, and we ourselves noticed how willingly and politely they accepted a "Gospel" offered to them in the trains and tramcars, while some English fellows turn away with a mutter that sounds like first cousin to an oath if you offer them the words of eternal life.

The Young Women's Christian Association, under the presidency of Mrs. Barnett, is a great boon in the city, and much good is being done through this department of Christian work.

[1] Rev. J. W. Fleming, B.D.

At the United Thanksgiving Service the hall was crowded to excess—a sight which cheered the praying Christians whose hearts had throbbed with holy desire that the country should be aroused. One editor reports that this and the testimony meeting which followed were "scenes that have never before been witnessed in Buenos Ayres."

ALAMEDA.

A correspondent, in writing to the magazine of the South American Missionary Society, says :—

The closing night came all too soon ; the Hall was filled, and we noticed those who had come from Rosario, Campana, Quilmes, Lomas, Temperley, Las Flores, Tandil, etc., some having travelled hundreds of miles to be present—a fact which speaks for itself. Mr. Grubb held in his hand a number of letters from those who had attended the meetings, testifying to blessings received. He remarked that only a quarter of them were from women. As time did not permit of all being read, Mr. Grubb selected a few (39) of these testimonies, which were listened to with much interest. All seemed to be full of praise and thanksgiving.

C

From the testimonies it was evident that before the mission many had only trusted the Lord Jesus to save them from hell, but during the mission had learned that we have a Saviour who wants to keep us from sinning, and even to take the desire for all that is contrary to His will right out of us. Now Jesus is saving some " to the uttermost," and no wonder that shouts of praise have gone up to Him out of full hearts. Many, too, have learned to pray as never before. These prayer meetings, generally conducted by our dear brother Millard, were characterised by intense earnestness and absence of all formality, hence no wonder the answers which were obtained and the blessing following.

There is, however, a sad side to be narrated. The hand of the LORD moved several times as a danger signal, so that men might be turned from their evil ways, and henceforth live not "unto themselves, but unto Him which died for them and rose again" (2 Cor. v. 15). Serious accidents occurred on the polo ground and football field on Sundays; three of these proved fatal, and in one case death took place almost instantaneously.

What other interpretation can be given than that it is the voice, the cry, the thunder-roll of the ALMIGHTY, a triple warning to the GOD-forgetting, self-pleasing, and soul-neglecting English—Christian—community !

"Now is the accepted time."

"The night cometh."

"Be ye therefore ready."

## CHAPTER IV.

ROSARIO DE SANTA FÉ is situated up the river from Buenos Ayres, about eight hours' run by the Argentine Railway. On our way there we broke the journey for one service at Campana, a

SOUTH-EASTERN ENTRANCE TO CENTRAL ARGENTINE RAILWAY, ROSARIO.

small town noted chiefly for its meat freezing works. Two Christian men, one employed on the railway and the other in the meat freezing works, conduct services every week in a room lent for the purpose by the railway company, and have sought to lift up CHRIST and Him crucified to the people around, both Spanish and English.

There are also a few members of the Salvation Army, whose devotion has been owned of GOD to the conversion of souls.

We were encouraged by joining in prayer with these earnest Christians. About fifty people attended at the meeting which they had arranged. The power of GOD accompanied His own word, and men and women were drawn nigh unto Him.

Rosario is quite a large town, possessing an English community, a Church of England chaplaincy, church and schoolroom in the same compound; also a Wesleyan chapel and a Seamen's Home and Mission. We found three licensed lay - readers, who are also accustomed to read the Church of England service, and conduct Sunday-school at the railway work-shops. During our stay a decided revival broke out in Rosario. The whole of the

THE MILKMAN AT THE DOOR, CAMPANA

community was stirred to its depths, and some who were living entirely for the world felt so profoundly the emptiness of their lives that they could not sleep at night.

A glance at the monthly record of the church (St. Bartholomew's) showed that the Rosario Christians, like those in Buenos Ayres, as well as too many in England itself, relied upon worldly means for supporting "Church work."

A bazaar is common enough, with its articles for sale, too often as useless as they are fabulous in price; but when one reads that so many dollars were received as payment for the hire of the church schoolroom for a Cinderella dance, one might well ask, "What next?"

Well, the next thing was a dance arranged on the middle night of the Mission, and the clergyman of the parish proposed, that as this date had been fixed before the Mission was announced, we should close the church on that night, so as not to give any offence to the members of the congregation.

When this sort of thing happens, no wonder that the congregation needs reviving! One shrinks from criticising, but there are so many inexcusable instances of every sort of worldliness in the Church at the present day, that it is absolutely necessary for some one to protest. I therefore throw up my visor and speak boldly.

Clergymen, ministers, laymen, and lady missionaries are wanted for South America, but men are not wanted who merely "go through services," and do not preach the Gospel. Such words may appear to show a spirit of "judgment," but as the object of these pages is to persuade men to come to this continent to preach the Gospel, it is of the utmost importance that this should be clearly understood, and that those sent out should be men who know and obey the Gospel.[1] St. Paul was able to say that he "kept back nothing that was profitable." When about to go to Jerusalem, he said with confidence to those among whom he had been preaching the kingdom of God, "I take you to record this day, that I am pure from the blood of all

[1] See pages 54, 55.

men. For I have not shunned to declare unto you ALL *the counsel of* GOD."
(Acts xx. 20, 26, 27.) And again, in writing to the Thessalonian Christians,
he said, "We preached unto you the Gospel of GOD, and ye are witnesses,
and GOD also, how *holily* and *justly* and *unblameably* we behaved ourselves
among you that believe."

Are we to be satisfied with anything short of this? GOD forbid!

When the Gospel, the full Gospel, is preached, hungry souls flock to the
feet of JESUS; and those who have been bound down with besetting sins,

CENTRAL ARGENTINE RAILWAY WORKS.

like fetters of iron, cry out to the Risen LORD to snap the chain and set the
captive free; while others, surrounded with the frightful temptations of life,
find in Him an abiding Friend and Keeper.

The dance "came off," but to the utter astonishment of many the church
was well filled notwithstanding, and there are some who from that night praise
the LORD that the love of the FATHER has cast out the love of the world.

The morning prayer meetings in the vestry were solemn and earnest,
while the Bible expositions in the church in the afternoons for Christians
might have been described as rich unfoldings of the Word of God. The

evening services were chiefly evangelistic, frequently followed by an after-meeting; and day after day souls were born again, and Christians led on to a deeper spiritual life and a closer walk with GOD.

The railway workshops are at Talleres Huevos, about two miles from the town of Rosario, where three meetings were held daily for the men employed at the works, and for their wives and children.

The cottage meetings for mothers were seasons of great blessing; some doubting ones trusted CHRIST, and the tongues of the dumb were made to sing. The children were addressed at the close of school, when a good many were led to look to JESUS as their SAVIOUR. For the evening services we were allowed to have the clerks' offices of the locomotive department, when the desks were pushed back and chairs arranged. The LORD was present in power, and wrought great wonders in the hearts of many.

One morning a woman, a notoriously troublesome person, met me, and with a shining face said, "I've got now what I've been longing for for twenty years!"

"What is that?" said I.

"Deliverance," she replied. "Many a time have I asked for the needed pardon, but only to go and fall again, bringing more misery to my wretched home; but when you spoke about the blood of JESUS being able to cleanse us from all sin, I said, '*That's what I want.*' So I trusted the LORD, and He has delivered me."

Her husband, too, gave

MR. AND MRS. A. B. COOK AND BRO. T. G. RUSSELL GOING TO SERVICE ON SUNDAY EVENING NEAR FISHERTON.

his heart to the LORD, and on the third night their eldest son, a boy of sixteen, remained behind with three other lads seeking salvation. All four found CHRIST that night, and before going away asked if they might have a special meeting for their mates the next day. It was so arranged, and when the time came, fourteen turned up, some coming straight from the shops in their working clothes, black and oily. It was a lovely sight to us, as at the close of the meeting eight of them found the LORD. These, with the previous four, made a company of twelve disciples. We have since heard that they are still going ahead, and that the men and women also have, of their own freewill, continued their week-night meeting, and with added blessing. The wife of "Tom the Blacksmith," in whose cottage I stayed for the eight days, writes :—

"Twelve of the boys went out one Sunday into the 'camp' (open country) with their hymn-books and Bibles. Choosing a spot near a brick-kiln, they began to sing, read, and pray. The owner of the kiln, a Spaniard, hearing the sound of voices, came out and asked them what they were doing. They told him, and to their delight he said, 'You can come here whenever you like, and you may have this place for your meeting.'"

One of the lads also wrote testifying to the blessing they had received, while another one suggested a new version of Hymn No. 350 in Songs and Solos :—

> "I feel like singing all the time,
> My heart is flowing o'er ;
> For JESUS is a Friend of mine,
> I'll never sin no more !"

"Whosoever is born of GOD doth not commit sin" (1 John iii. 8). Would to GOD every Christian grasped the truth that the LORD wishes to save us, so that we may not go on committing sin.

The power of GOD silenced all criticism, and the remark made by one of the lay-readers at the closing meeting, as he listened to the vocal testimonies of one and another, was : "If you had described such a scene as this last week, I would have said 'Impossible !'" And so it is impossible with man, but "with GOD all things are possible," and "all things are possible to him that believeth."

The revival spread into the Seamen's Home, where two earnest Christians are labouring. Perhaps it will not be out of place here to state that the Rev. Edward W. Matthew's visit to South America, in 1890, was greatly blessed of God, not only to Rosario, when this Mission was established, but to Buenos Ayres, Campana, and Monte Video. Mr. Spooner, the harbour Missionary at Rosario, writes :—

*Seamen's Home and Mission,*
*148, Calle Progreso,*
*Rosario,*
*July 29, 1893.*

ROSARIO SEAMEN'S HOME MISSION.[1]

" I must give vent to what is uppermost in my mind—viz., the visit of Mr. Grubb and his Mission party to Rosario, which has proved a real blessing, and to the Home especially. Our hearts had been going up to GOD, and He has made our cup to run over. My dear wife and I have been greatly helped and refreshed, and our two eldest daughters have passed from death unto life, and three of our helpers at the Home have been converted, and two backsliders restored ; so, with the sailors and others staying with us in the house, who have professed faith in CHRIST, some *fourteen souls received blessing in the Home.* A good number in Rosario have come in for blessing, and many of GOD's children have been refreshed and strengthened with Divine power for fuller consecration to the Master's service.

" We rejoice exceedingly that our English Consul has come out boldly for CHRIST, and many at the Central Railway works have done likewise, and we are seeing others coming on the LORD's side day by day, and we expect still greater things."

---

[1] Kindly lent from the Society's Sailors Magazine, *Chart and Compass,* which now has a wide circulation in the chief ports of South America. The Society is working in five of the principal ports.

The spiritual life of many Englishmen who own land in the interior, living with their families on estancias, is very often at a terribly low ebb. Shut off by many miles of flat, treeless, uninteresting " camp," from any other human beings, men grow sadly careless—labour being scarce, gentlemen's sons live a hardy life here, working like ordinary farm labourers. Exposed to the air and heat of the sun, they look physically robust : but many confess

AN ESTANCIA NEAR PELIGRINI, ARGENTINA.

that it cannot be said of them, that they are " in health even as their soul prospereth "; but if their souls' health prospered as gloriously as their bodies, then God's name would be honoured indeed, and His presence known among them.

Flying visits to some of these farms were, thank God, blessed to not a few, and we have since heard that family prayers have been revived, and that some are again enjoying " the peace of God," which they had lost through neglect of communion with the Lord and of the study of His Word.

The town of Cordoba was the farthest point inland reached in this tour.

It is said that Cordoba is the most advanced Roman Catholic community in the Republic.

Mr. Robison, a lawyer from Sydney, N.S.W., who had joined our party in Buenos Ayres, accompanied Mr. Grubb for a short stay there.  His account reads as follows :—

*Monday.*—We left Rosario by the 6.30 p.m. train.  The country through which we passed was uniformly flat, and parched-looking.  Every here and there we noticed estancias, and dotted about along the rail track were native huts, with dirty-looking men and women in the doorway, evidently called out for the event of the day,—viz., the passing of the train.  Close along the line lay bleaching skeletons of cattle and sheep.

About 8.30 a.m. we reached Cordoba, and were there welcomed by three gentlemen, who we soon learned were the representatives of the small body of English-speaking people in Cordoba—numbering at most one hundred souls, while the total population of the city amounts to somewhere near forty thousand.  We asked the guidance of the HOLY SPIRIT that we might make the most of the short time at our disposal, and felt led to announce a list of services.

Notices having been put up, we sallied forth to see something of the city, and being directed to a mound on the outskirts, from which a good view could be obtained, we made our way thither and poured out our hearts to GOD for Cordoba.

On all sides we saw large buildings, many of them evidently of considerable age and grandeur.  The number of Roman Catholic churches deeply impressed us.  There was not one of any other denomination, but on all sides popish domes and spires rose.  On making inquiry we were told there were no less than fifteen, in addition to the convents and monasteries in which the nuns and priests are trained.  Leaving our " little hill," we went into the city and entered one of the least remarkable churches.  The roof was a mass of gold, while the walls were simply covered with pictures, shrines, and images, with candles burning before them.  It was my first experience of public idolatry, and I shall never forget it.  With a prayer that the LORD would throw the true Light into the dark hearts of the poor creatures kneeling before the shrines, we left.

YOUNG LION, ARGENTINA.

CHURCH OF SAN DOMINGO, CORDOBA.

We heard afterwards that in the church of San Domingo there is a renowned image, called the "*Virgin of the Miracles*," which is supposed to have the power of performing miraculous cures. Once each year this image is carried forth, and a procession made through the principal streets of the city. Upon this occasion numbers of people come from great distances to obtain a glimpse, and seek "*the blessing of the virgin.*"

THE MIRACULOUS VIRGIN.

The remainder of the day was spent in quietly waiting upon GOD. About forty came to the first service, which was held in a small hall fitted up and kept by the little band of English-speaking people. They meet together every Sunday, and, as there has been no clergyman or minister in Cordoba for some years, one of their number reads the Church of England service. The old story of the love of CHRIST appeared new to many as Mr. Grubb quietly spoke to them.

The following day, both at the children's service and at the evening meeting, many souls yielded to CHRIST for the first time. One Roman Catholic doctor came to Mr. Grubb after the evening meeting, and clasping him by the hand said, with tears in his eyes,—

"Thank you, sir, indeed, for what you have said to-night! It is the first common-sense sermon I have ever heard."

Our final service the following day, held just two hours before our train started, was well attended, although in the busy part of the day ; and we left feeling that He who had promised that His word shall not return unto Him void would indeed accomplish much with the seed sown in His name.

It was here that we met Mr. Payne, who had been a Missionary both in Ireland and Spain, and who now is travelling through the interior of South America with his Bible Carriage. He told a pitiful tale of the *needs of inland parts*, how for months he travelled and never came across *one* who knew anything of the love of CHRIST.

"My brethren, *these things* ought not so to be" (James iii. 10).

# CHAPTER V.

VIEW OF THE LITTLE HILL FROM THE ROOF OF A HOUSE.

MONTEVIDEO is situated in the province of Uruguay, at the mouth of the River Plate (which at this point is said to be one hundred and fifty miles wide), and is in communication with Buenos Ayres by a steam packet service, which runs two steamers across the river during the twenty-four hours. The name Montevideo means "I see a mountain" (a striking occurrence in this part of the country), there being a little hill here five hundred feet above sea level.

The town boasts of an English community and church, and an American Methodist chapel, where combined English and Spanish congregations meet for worship.

According to the *Church Magazine*, many departments of work are undertaken, and numerous services conducted, with baptisms, marriages, and burials.

A converted verger is a very rare plant, but we were encouraged to meet with a specimen here, though not surprised to find that he had been brought to the LORD through the instrumentality of the Salvation Army. He met us on the boat, and escorted us cheerfully, and with a "Praise the LORD," to our appointed quarters.

HOLY TRINITY CHURCH, MONTEVIDEO.

At 8 p.m. the same evening we assembled in the vestry of Holy Trinity Church for a prayer meeting, at which there were twelve present, including the two ministers of the American Methodist Episcopal Church.

The clergyman of the parish being away on furlough, his place was being filled by a *locum tenens* who was otherwise engaged, so could not be with us.

That prayer meeting we ourselves shall never forget, for the LORD's presence was so wonderfully real, and prayer flowed freely. We were led by the HOLY SPIRIT to ask for blessing far and wide, and when pleading for the spread of the Gospel in the country, our eyes were opened and we saw with unmistakable clearness of vision the whole of the neglected continent aglow with the fire of GOD through the name of JESUS. Our own hearts were filled afresh with the HOLY GHOST, and our faith strengthened to believe that the day is not far distant when the devil's kingdom shall be consumed, and the GOD of Heaven set up a Kingdom which shall never be destroyed, but stand for ever (Dan. ii. 44).

The Sunday services were conducted in the church, where Mr. Grubb preached both morning and evening, while an address was given to the Sunday scholars in the Lafone Hall, which proved to be "a time of salvation" for the children.

The work among the Spaniards, under the American Methodist Episcopal Church, is encouraging, but owing to the *lack of workers* it makes what is done appear only "a drop in a bucket," for there are 750,000 souls in this the smallest province of South America.

Leaving Montevideo by steamer, we proceeded to RIO DE JANEIRO, and spent the four days on the water in close communion with GOD. The second day was a Sunday, and the devil showed fight in many ways. Reports having reached the passengers that "a warm time might be expected if Mr. Grubb preached on board," they acted accordingly. The rule of the ship's company, that when a clergyman is on board he is to be asked to conduct the service, was totally ignored, and at the appointed time, when the bell rang, the people assembled in the saloon, the captain himself "did duty."

He galloped through the Prayers, dashed over the *Venite*, and raced down the Collects with astonishing speed, completing the last one at a hundred yards' pace, without taking breath, closed with the Benediction, shut up the book, and the "whole thing" was over in nineteen minutes! The sailors and stewards regarded this with indifference, and on inquiry we found that it was the usual thing when the captain took service. Our steward being a Christian, we had good times with him, as also with some of the steerage passengers.

Two days later we called at Santos, noted for its coffee export. The scenery in the harbour was beyond description in grandeur and beauty, but we heard sad tales of numerous deaths through the outbreak of yellow fever in the town. Not long since a whole ship's crew was carried off in the course of one month while the vessel was in port.

Rio de Janeiro can be reached from here by rail, travelling *vià* São Paulo, a city of 50,000 inhabitants; but we completed the journey by steamer, and the next day entered Rio harbour—the most beautiful in the world.

ENTRANCE TO RIO HARBOUR.

## CHAPTER VI.

THE ENTRANCE OF THE BAY OF RIO DE JANEIRO, viewed from the deck of a steamer, looks extremely narrow, owing to the sugar-loaf peak which rises abruptly from the sea on the left, to a height of 1,212 feet; while on the right, and built up from the water's edge, stands the fortress of Santa Cruz—the most formidable in all Brazil.

The actual width is said to be about one mile; it is very straight, and the course so clear that no pilots are necessary.

Once inside the bay, a feeling of wonderful safety from the storms of the Atlantic comes over one, for there is the calm of a summer sea, and the high granite mountain chains shelter it in every direction. Near at hand, the bare grey peaks huddle together about the entrance, as if to drive back the ocean tempest; while straight ahead the eye is relieved by the ever-green slopes and ragged profile of the far-famed Organ Mountains. The bay is sixteen miles long and eleven wide, with one hundred islands, and forms the debouchure of twenty little rivers. Multitudes of steamships and sailing vessels, flying the colours of almost every nation, are seen riding at anchor, and paddle ferries flitting across its surface.

MAIL BOAT ENTERING RIO HARBOUR.

Steam launches and ordinary rowing boats convey passengers to the mainland, the shores of the bay being too shallow for ocean-going steamers to come alongside the landing stages.

The population, estimated at over 300,000, is chiefly composed of Portuguese and Brazilians, though there is a proportion of blacks, and a decidedly "mixed multitude."

There are about 2,000 English-speaking people in Rio and its suburbs, but their houses are scattered all round the bay, so that comparatively few could, if they wished, attend the English church on Sundays.

Christ Church, which is wholly dependent upon local support, was the first Protestant church erected in South America. It was built in 1810, on the conditions that it had the outward appearance of a private house, and that no bell should be used.

The chaplain invited Mr. Grubb to preach here on the first Sunday morning. A fair congregation assembled to take part in the Mission; but the general tone of the English community might be summed up in the remark of one conservative individual, which was to this effect:—

THE PALM GROVE, BOTANICAL GARDENS.
*From a Photograph by Marc Ferrez.*

> Missions may come, and Missions may go,
> With what result I do not know;
> Excitement has its ebb and flow,
> But I go on for ever.

The American missionaries, however, were much more enthusiastic, and received the suggestion of some revival services, among both the English and Portuguese, with outstretched arms.

Prayer meetings in English were held at noon every day in the offices of the Rev. H. C. Tucker (Secretary of the American Bible Society there), and English services were conducted every evening in the American Methodist Church.

As many Portuguese and Brazilian Christians desired to share in the blessing, the time was divided between the American Presbyterian Mission and the Mission called the "*Igreja Evangelica Fluminense*," or perhaps better known as Dr. Kalley's Church, named after the Scotch physician who, in 1858, so nobly started work here. The Portuguese congregations were, of course, addressed through an interpreter. Many of the Christians were greatly refreshed, and some halting believers helped into the Kingdom. There is also an old-established

Portuguese church in connection with Rio, situated across the bay at a place called Nictheroy. Here the pastor is the Rev. Leonidas Silva, who was in England some years at "Harley House" College, under Dr. Grattan Guinness.

The Rio "Seamen's Beth-el" is under the charge of two[1] workers, one belonging to the South American Missionary Society. Their hearts have been often cheered by seeing souls saved; but it is not an easy matter to get into contact with naval men, who are not allowed on shore after dusk, because of the immoral state of the city. We could not help praising GOD, however, for this rule, as no sooner has the sun gone down, than those who "love darkness rather than light because their deeds are evil," sally forth or stand at their doorways seeking to catch their prey, and already "many strong men have been slain."

THE LATE Dr. K. R. KALLEY.

The Brazilian YOUNG MEN'S CHRISTIAN ASSOCIATION, which has only a short while been inaugurated, is making rapid strides. At a special evan-

[1] Mr. H. Brandreth, of the South American Missionary Society, and Mr. Williams, of the "*Wesson*" Mission to Seamen, both having their respective local Managing Committees.

gelistic meeting in the Dr. Kalley Church, no less than 125 men were present. Some of these, of course, were only casual attendants; but it gave one an idea of the opportunity for men to labour here, if they are only willing to step into South America at the command of the King. The meeting was very solemn, and before the close special prayer was offered for Brazil, and GOD gave us the assurance that there was one of their number specially chosen of GOD for work in that province.

LE CORCOVADO.

*Photograph by Marc Ferrez.*

Mr. Clarke is the Secretary, and has been wonderfully taught of the LORD in the Portuguese language, the testimony of some of the older missionaries being that, "considering the short time he has been studying the language, he speaks with remarkable fluency." *But he is almost single-handed.* Although the work among the young men has a very hopeful side, it must ever be remembered that *more men are wanted* to witness among them.

The power of evil is not to be under-rated, neither is the weakness of many backboneless young men to be forgotten; at the same time let us not limit the power of "the HOLY ONE of Israel" (Ps. lxxviii. 41).

"For He is Almighty, yes, He is Almighty;
Almighty to save and to keep."

If the devil is able to get these men to serve him, surely GOD the HOLY

GHOST can bring their hearts into subjection to His will, and so win them over to the Kingdom of GOD that they will fight bravely, and with a "free will," under His banner of love.

There is a Brazilian Club in Rio, for young men, the members of which wage war under the name of "*Tenentes do Diabo*," or the "Lieutenants of the Devil." The following cutting from the leading newspaper recently announced a grand picnic to be given by these young men. From all accounts, the "*Tenentes do Diabo*" serve their captain faithfully. They behave diabolically, flinging themselves whole-heartedly into the pleasures of the world and the flesh. We were told that on carnival days they dress up in red tights, horns, and long tails, and drive up and down the public streets in open carriages, ending the day by beginning a night of unrestrained debauch. Maddened by satanic excitement, they throw the reins on the neck of passion, and spur themselves on, down, down, down the broad road, and on to an open hell.

These are not ashamed to make fools of themselves in the service of sin, and yet how many professed soldiers of the Cross are ashamed to be seen in the regimentals of "the KING's own," with "the high praises of GOD in their mouth and a two-edged sword in their hand" (Psalm cxlix. 6)!

**T. D.**

S. E. COMMERCIAL

**TENENTES DO DIABO**

DOMINGO, 14 DE AGOSTO DE 1892

**GRANDE PASSEIO**
**MARITIMO E CAMPESTRE**

DE

**INICIATIVA**

á pittoresca e aprazivel ilha de Paquetá

**SUMPTUOSO PIC-NIC**

E

magnificas regatas gentilmente
organizadas pelo distincto

**GRUPO DOS CANOTIERS**

A commissão promotora desta festa é
encontrada na CAVERNA todas as noites
das 8 ás 10 horas, á disposição dos Srs
socios, quer para cartões de cavalheiros
quer para Exmas. familias.

O 1º SECRETARIO DA COMMISSÃO,

**GOMES DA SILVA.**

The Romish Church here seems to an outsider to be in so shameful a condition, that public delineation is impossible ; while a description of the lives of some of the priests would be soiling to the mind to narrate, and too poisonous to read.

In a paper giving the aims of the South American Missionary Society, we read :—

One of the objects of this Society is to carry on work among the Roman Catholic population and immigrants of various nationalities. Some have sought out the Society's Chaplains and Lay Missionaries for information and guidance, attended services held in their own languages, and sent their children to the Society's Schools. The Society's Chaplains and Lay Agents are expected not only to be accessible to all inquirers after truth, but to acquire the languages of the different countries, and to read, expound, and distribute the Holy Scriptures to the people as opportunity offers, and to establish Sunday Schools for the young and periodical services for adults wherever practicable.

Would to GOD a revival in this department might be made, for, as far as we were able to judge, there is next to nothing done in this direction. Alas ! too many, both in England and abroad, entertain the idea that " Rome is a sister Church in error." As a matter of fact, *here* it is ABSOLUTE HEATHENISM.

A correspondent from another Brazilian town bears testimony to this statement.

1893. *1st October.*—The need out here seems to me to be greater than ever. The more one looks into the state of things in this land the more appalling it appears. Every little mud hut has its household altar, with its images and saints. Romanism here is another name for Heathenism : its followers are none the less idolaters. " CHRIST" is often held up to the people, but, alas! it is a brass CHRIST on a bronze cross! There are many saints here, but they are made of wood and metal! Just to-day I saw a spectacle that made me feel sick at heart. It was a so-called religious procession. In front were a few men with silver or silvered lanterns, some with lighted candles, then came a silvered crucifix, then a large rough painted image—I think it was intended for the virgin and the Child JESUS; afterwards quite a number of little human representations of angels, with muslin dresses, silvered

A BRAZILIAN HOMESTEAD.

crowns, and tinsel wings, etc., etc. At home it might pass well in some circus during the New Year week, but here it makes you feel like weeping for the poor blind sheep, and your righteous indignation rises against these feeders on the fleece of the flock. Oh! when shall the Church of CHRIST arise to see the hollow mockery, the carnal sham, the pitiable imitation of religious truths that garnish the outside of Rome, which within is full of rottenness and dead men's bones!

A spirit of false toleration even creeps over the hearts of workers in the field, unless kept by the power of GOD. One of the Missionaries at a prayer meeting asked for a revival in his own spiritual life, and, afterwards taking me on one side, he said :—

"Brother, some time ago I read an account of the work in which Mr. Grubb and his co-workers were engaged, in visiting Mission Stations, and the thought passed through my mind that it was strange to go on '*a Mission to Missionaries*,' for I thought that living in the very midst of the great field of heathenism, one would surely be kept up by the sight of the appalling need before one's very eyes. Now that I have had this experience myself, I see it is not the sight of the need that gives power to the faint, but that all supply must be drawn from GOD Himself. There may be many others who have been deceived in the same way."

The Thanksgiving Service at the close of the Mission was held in the American Methodist Episcopal Church in Largo do Cattete, when the building was crowded, every seat occupied, and many persons standing.

Having been announced as "*a United Meeting*," people of every Church and nationality came. Black, dark brown, light brown, yellow, pale and white-faced men, women, and children streamed in. Some of the English and American young men who had been blessed during the week were over-flowing with joy. The sight was truly one for great rejoicing. Once again were we permitted to see man-made barriers thrown down, and every heart caused to realize the truth that we are all one in CHRIST JESUS. After a most stirring service, with an address by interpretation, one of the missionaries asked all present who had received blessing during the Mission to testify to the fact by rising in their seats, and to publicly thank GOD for His out-poured SPIRIT.

Fully three hundred rose to their feet, choruses of praise were sung, and all rejoiced together that the Giver of every good and perfect gift had thus "opened His hand and filled them with good." Yes, "good measure, pressed down and running over."

# CHAPTER VII

REST HOUSE, VIEWED FROM
YERS' WALK, BAHIA.

BAHIA is called " *the bay of all the saints*," on account of every church being dedicated to some Romish saint : and as it so happens, the theatres are all similarly distinguished.

The town is prettily situated on the sides and summit of a range of hills, and when viewed from the bay has a formidable appearance, as the land rises almost perpendicularly from the shore ; so much so, that a gigantic hydraulic lift, and a dangerously steep cable tram, are used to convey the inhabitants from the lower to the upper part of the town.

The streets are narrow and eastern-looking, with a mule tram-service throughout. The public buildings, offices, and shops are whitewashed, and consequently very dazzling under the tropical sun.

Water is supplied chiefly from wells, one of these which we passed having a drinking fountain also. Mules are used to carry the firkins to and from the wells, though women at times may be seen with one upon their heads.

A short ride by mule tram out of the town brings one into the most beautiful country. Both for foliage and general appearance, it resembles the loveliest spots in Ceylon. The Rev. and Mrs. Chamberlain gave us an invitation to meet at their house, with the English chaplain, a Baptist missionary, and a lay worker. We gladly accepted, and though our stay on shore

MULES LADEN WITH FRESH WATER AT THE WELL, BAHIA, BRAZIL.

could only be a few hours at the most, we thank GOD for this visit. The time was spent in prayer and the most earnest conversation, and we were intensely interested in hearing of the hunger for His word that GOD is creating in the hearts of the priest-ridden natives.

The same old story of European vice, however—to say nothing of spiritual indifference—had to be repeated here ; and although there are, praise GOD, some Englishmen who seek to live straight lives, the aspect of

things was not very bright. We easily judged for ourselves in what light
the natives regard the presence of " English" (who continually go ashore
from the steamers that call there), by the invitations we received, when
passing through the lower part of the town, from young boys, who were
desirous of guiding us to houses of very questionable reputation, as they
addressed us with, " Eng-
lish, come this side." Shame,
shame, thrice shame upon
us, that Christian England
should leave such impressions
among a practically heathen
people!

A day and a night steaming
farther north brought us to
PERNAMBUCO. The mail-
packets anchor about three
miles from the shore, and as
the weather is frequently
stormy at this, the most eastern port of Brazil, passengers
are not always able to leave
or join the ship. A coral reef
forms the harbour of Pernambuco, and, as may be seen

THE AGENT'S BOAT OFF PERNAMBUCO.

from the picture, has a lighthouse erected at the northern end.

Yellow fever rages here not infrequently, and we heard that within one
month, during the early part of this year, no less than twelve English resi-
dents, including the English chaplain, fell victims to this terrible scourge.
The case of the chaplain was exceptionally heart-rending, as he had only
been joined by his wife and children three days previously.

One of the Protestant Portuguese Churches here is in connection with the Dr. Kalley Church in Rio de Janeiro, and has benefited much from the labours of Pastor James Fanstone. Although the steamer was only delayed a few hours, a meeting was arranged for in this church, when Mr. Grubb preached, Mr. Maxwell Wright[1] acting as interpreter.

A letter received from Mr. McCall, dated February 24th, 1893, narrating his first impressions of the Romish land in which he was to labour, will give a fair idea of the character of the people and their need of the truth.

THE SQUARE, BAHIA.

"We arrived in Pernambuco on Sunday morning, and had to land or else go farther south. Reluctantly, therefore, we had to submit, and after much waiting got on shore just in time for the beginning of the three days' carnival.

"All over the city there were strings of streamers right across the roads. Business was going on just as if there were no Sabbath ; but towards the evening, processions of all kinds began to throng the streets, and as our service was being held in the Preaching Hall, the speaker had sometimes to stop - the noise outside was so great. Young men and women turned out by the thousands, I should think, dressed in all sorts of fantastic, diabolic, and lewd dresses ; beating drums, pans, etc. ; playing all kinds of musical and other instruments ; shouting, singing, yelling, screaming, leaping and dancing,—it seemed in real earnest as if the devil had been let loose for a season. This continued till Tuesday night, and seemed to get worse towards the close ; but now all is quiet again, as this is the holy season !

[1] See "Help for Brazil" (occasional paper) ; "To Brazil by Way of Madeira" (6d. Religious Tract Society of Scotland, Edinburgh).

"One feels like Jeremiah, 'Oh, that my head were waters, and mine eyes a fountain of tears, that I might weep day and night for the slain of the daughter of this people.' Truly the God of this world hath blinded their eyes.

"GOD has used all this in giving me a love for these dear, dark souls. This religious slavery and Romish ecclesiastical phosphorus seems the masterpiece of Satan to blind souls to the true light which now shineth. . . ."

Are these things to remain so? Is the evil one to sway his sceptre over this vast continent without rebuke?

Nay, verily!

But where are the men and women who are willing and ready at the KING'S command to ride fearlessly into the enemy's country, to throw down the gauntlet in the name of JESUS?

The cry of many a Spirit-moved heart goes up to the throne of GOD, "Willing; yes; willing."

But "who is sufficient for these things?" For we are not ignorant of his devices.

The answer, uttered by the Apostle Paul himself, sounds deep, clear, and strong, as the echo comes rolling down the ages,—"Our sufficiency is of GOD."

### What is the Bible definition of THE GOSPEL ?

The Angel said unto the shepherds (Luke ii. 10), " FEAR NOT : for, behold, I bring you GOOD TIDINGS of GREAT JOY, which shall be to all people. For unto you is born this day in the City of David a SAVIOUR, which is CHRIST the LORD."

(*a*) " SAVIOUR " = One who saves.—Saves the lost.—Not a helper, to assist
　(which is)　　　the sinner to save himself.

(*b*) " CHRIST " = GOD'S anointed One.
　　　　　　　Not a human discovery ; but a Divine appoint-
　(the)　　　ment.

(*c*) " LORD " = All powerful One.
　　　　　　　Not one who is merely stronger than the sinner ;
　　　　　　　but who is able to save to the uttermost.

" GO YE INTO ALL THE WORLD, AND PREACH THE GOSPEL
TO EVERY CREATURE."

Glad news ! good tidings of great joy ! for here is a Saviour of God's appointment, who is able to save. Hallelujah !

We are not told to preach sermons ; but we are told to preach CHRIST.

When our LORD gave His parting words to His disciples, He said : " Ye shall receive power, after the HOLY GHOST is come upon you : and ye shall be witnesses unto ME (witnesses unto a person) both in Jerusalem, Judæa, Samaria, and unto the uttermost parts of the earth " (Acts i. 8).

Thus it is clear that we are to preach CHRIST the SAVIOUR, LORD. Preach and witness unto *Him* Who is able to save to the uttermost, and this Gospel of good tidings is to be preached unto " ALL PEOPLE " (Luke ii. 10).

" An uttermost SAVIOUR "
" For the uttermost parts."

### What is the Apostolic Example?

"They therefore that were scattered abroad went about *preaching the word*" (Acts viii. 4, R.V.).

"Philip went down to the city of Samaria, and *preached unto them* THE CHRIST" (Acts viii. 5, R.V.).

"They believed Philip preaching good tidings concerning the Kingdom of God and THE NAME *of* JESUS CHRIST" (Acts viii. 12, R.V.).

"Peter and John, when they had testified and *preached the word of the* LORD, returned to Jerusalem, and *preached the gospel* in many villages of the Samaritans" (Acts viii. 25).

"Philip," when sent by the Spirit to the Ethiopian eunuch in the desert, "*preached unto him* JESUS" (Acts viii. 35).

"Philip was found at Azotus: and passing through, he *preached the* GOSPEL to all the cities, till he came to Cæsarea" (Acts viii. 40, R V.).

Paul, of whom the LORD said, "He is a chosen vessel unto ME, to *bear* MY NAME before the Gentiles, and Kings, and the Children of Israel," "*preached* CHRIST *in the Synagogues*" (Acts ix. 20).

Paul "*preached boldly in Damascus in* THE NAME OF JESUS" (Acts ix. 27).

Paul was with the disciples, "coming in and going out at Jerusalem, *preaching boldly in* THE NAME OF THE LORD" (Acts ix. 28, R.V.). Etc., etc., etc.

### There are only two religions in the World.
### The TRUE and the FALSE.

All the phases of false religion are alike. They all say :

"*Something* in my hand I bring."

The only difference between them being as to what that "something" is.

The TRUE Religion says :

"Nothing in my hand I bring."

---

Notes from a conversation with the Rev. E. W. Bullenger, D.D., at a missionary breakfast. See "Ten Sermons on the Second Advent," by Rev. E. W. Bullenger.

E.

"When the Rev. George W. Chamberlain first went to South America he found fifteen millions of people in a nominally Papal land, who scarcely knew what a Bible was. One old patriarch of fourscore years, to whom he gave a Portuguese New Testament and explained salvation by faith, said to him, 'Young man, this is what I have long been waiting to hear. But where was your father when my father was alive, that he never came to tell my father how to be saved?'

"Some such question as that we must all answer, if not before we die, then at the judgment seat of CHRIST."—DR. PIERSON : *The Greatest Work in the World.*

# The Neglected Continent.

## PART II.

Historical Sketch and Summary of Missionary Enterprise.

LUCY E. GUINNESS.

# The Neglected Continent.

**NOTE.**

THE SPIRITUAL NEEDS OF SOUTH AMERICA may be judged by the darkness of this map. All centres where American or European Protestant missionaries are stationed are shown by the white dots numbered to refer to the Key. (The boundaries of the fourteen States of South America are indicated in white, as also the principal rivers.)

All parts printed black are either Roman Catholic, heathen, or uninhabited.

The population of South America is estimated at 37,000,000. Of these probably less than 4,000,000 have been reached by the Gospel, leaving 33,000,000 wholly unevangelized.

## KEY TO THE BLACK MISSIONARY MAP OF S. AMERICA.

Date of Founding
Wk. in S. America.

1735. Moravian Missionary Society (9).
1815. West Indian Conference (Wesleyan) (11).
1821. London Missionary Society (12).
1824. British and Foreign Bible Society (14).
1836. American Methodist Episcopal North (5).
1840. Plymouth Brethren (16).
1844. South American Missionary Society (10).
1855. Dr. Kalley's Churches "Help for Brazil" (8).
1856. American Presbyterian (North and South) (2 and 3).
1861. Society for the Propagation of the Gospel (13).
1864. American Bible Society (15).
1873. American Methodist Episcopal, South (4).
1879. Southern Baptist Convention (1).
1880. Bishop Taylor's Mission (7).
1889. American Episcopal (6).
1889. Salvation Army.

# The Neglected Continent.

## PART II.

### CHAPTER I.

#### SOUTH AMERICA'S SPIRITUAL STORY.

"Though our task is not to bring all the world to CHRIST, our task is unquestionably to bring CHRIST to all the world."—A. J. GORDON, D.D.

FOUR thousand seven hundred miles long and over three thousand wide—a stupendous Continent, seven million square miles in area, nearly twice the size of Europe, containing one-eighth of the land surface of the globe, the most magnificent system of river drainage in the world, a coast line 18,000 miles long, and two rocky mountain-chains of extraordinary magnitude and sublimity, it lies away in the western seas, between the Pacific and the Atlantic—SOUTH AMERICA—well called from a spiritual standpoint, *the Neglected Continent.*

Extending in an unbroken line of 4,500 miles from Cape Horn to Panama, its Alpine altitudes tower above the clouds, "piled one upon another like the fabled pillars of heaven." Among them CHIMBORAZO on the Equator, crowned with eternal snows, lifts its frozen summit 21,420 feet above sea-level—over four miles high—equal to Mount Etna capped by the Peak of Teneriffe. "Its wide-stretching plateaux, almost immeasurable savannas, and mighty rivers rolling their majestic waters over the plains to the ocean, impress the mind with sensations of awe and astonishment. Placed amid the summits of its Andes, the European traveller seems as if lifted into a new horizon and surrounded by the ruined fragments of a superior world."

In the far north-east its tropic ORINOCO surpasses by 100 miles even the flood-tide of the Ganges. In the sub-tropic south, the LA PLATA, 150 miles wide as it sweeps into the sea, runs the length of the Thames ten times over and a hundred miles to spare, in its 2,200 mile course, and pours into the ocean more water than any other river in the world —but one. For South America possesses a mightier stream than these. The whole of France or of the Ottoman Empire might lie in the

lap of its monarch AMAZON, the largest river in the world, which, equalling
the Indus and the Nile put together, offers at least 25,000 miles of navigable
water-course in unbroken sequence from the sea to the base of the Andes.
From the matchless network of natural waterway the Amazon affords, it has
been called the Mediterranean of South America. The soil of its basin, one
to two million square miles in area, and fertile enough to supply the inhabitants
of the world with food, is for the most part covered by sombre primeval forest
—pathless, impenetrable—the largest extent of arboreal growth in the world.

TITICACA, the largest lake in the New World south of the St. Lawrence
basin, belongs to this stately and colossal continent. One hundred and
seventy miles long by seventy broad, with an area of 3,500 square miles, it
could float Cyprus, Crete, or Corsica at an altitude 200 feet above the summit of Mount Etna. Its lonely waters have no outlet to the sea, but are
guarded on their southern shores by gigantic ruins of a pre-historic empire—
palaces, temples, and fortresses—silent, mysterious monuments of a long-lost
golden age.

" *The whole earth is the Lord's !*" exclaimed Count Zinzendorf ; "*men's
souls are His. I am a debtor to all.*"

"All that hath life and breath, sing to the LORD !" cried David, sum-
moning the universe to praise its infinite CREATOR.

In the great Song of Redemption, the chorus of renewed humanity, can
the millions of a continent like this be dumb, and GOD not miss their jubila-
tion ?

Can one-eighth of the globe be left out of the reckoning of the coming
Kingdom of CHRIST? Can the spiritual state of its 37,000,000 people be
immaterial to Him ?

What is that state ?

Who are these people ?

What has been done to bring them " *into the way of peace* " ?

SOUTH AMERICA is divided into fourteen great countries, and includes representatives of almost every variety of race and language—from the degraded Fuegians of the Cape Horn, who, when discovered, had drifted so far from old-world traditions that they retained no word for GOD, and from the Indian tribes of "sad, calm aspect" scattered on the pampas plains, or among the virgin forests of the Amazons, up to the Anglo-Saxon and Latin leaders of civilization in the free Republics. The numerous Negroes and Quadroons of the north and central states stand next in the social scale to the Mestizoes, a mixed people of Spanish or Portuguese and Indian blood, the "sensuous and exuberant half-caste riff-raff" resulting from the mingling of the white and red races. Imported Chinese coolies, and foreigners from almost every country under heaven, drawn hither by the fabled silver wealth of Ecuador, Peru, and Bolivia, crowd the cities of the western seaboard. The Spanish and Portuguese element is politically dominant, while the "Red Men" constitute the main stock of the population.

Discovered by the Portuguese Pedro Cabral A.D. 1500, SOUTH AMERICA has for nearly 400 years been part of the parish of the Pope. In contrast with it, the North of the New World — Puritan, prosperous, powerful, progressive—presents probably the most remarkable evidence earth affords of the blessing of Protestantism. For the results of ROMAN CATHOLICISM *left to itself*, are writ large in letters of gloom across the priest-ridden, lax, superstitious South. Her cities "among the gayest and grossest in the world," her ecclesiastics, enormously wealthy and strenuously opposed to progress and liberty, South America groans under the tyranny of a priesthood which in its highest forms is unillumined by and incompetent to preach the Gospel of God's free gift, and in its lowest is proverbially and "habitually drunken, extortionate, and ignorant." The fires of her unspeakable Inquisition still burn in the hearts of her ruling clerics, and although the spirit of the age has in our nineteenth century transformed all her Monarchies into Republics, Ecuador still prohibits any but Romish worship, and religious intolerance largely prevails.

"HER UNSPEAKABLE INQUISITION." [1]

Only the fringe of this Continent—more than sixty times as large as the United Kingdom, more than thirty times larger than Spain and Portugal, more than seven times larger than all British India—has been touched by the message of Free Salvation. On the frozen rocks of Fuegia, 43 years ago, Allen Gardiner and his noble band of companions (to whose labours the South American Missionary Society have since succeeded) kindled a spiritual beacon-light that to-day shines right round the world. Four thousand miles away in the deadly tropics of Guiana the heroic Moravian brethren died and

---

[1] The above illustration is a facsimile of that in Limborch's celebrated "*History of the Inquisition*" (vol. ii. p. 222).

died, till deathless blessing for multitudes sprang from their graves ; both extremes of the Continent thus proving the lowest of earth's races capable of becoming new creatures in JESUS CHRIST. Between these two extremities sixteen different missionary agencies have undertaken labour in this great harvest field. Their entire efforts are represented on our map on page 68.

By those efforts judge whether or no SOUTH AMERICA spiritually merits the title 'Neglected Continent.'

Omitting the group of Christian Churches in the Guianas on the north-east coast, and the scattered centres on the Atlantic borders of Brazil, one may say that *South America as a whole is almost untouched by aggressive Protestant missionary effort.*

Glance at its Republics, commencing at the North.

**VENEZUELA,** with an area of 593,943 square miles, more than nine times as large as England and Wales, and two and a half times larger than Germany, and *with a population of 2,200,000, has only one Protestant missionary.*

**COLOMBIA** area, 504,773 sq. m.), larger than the total area of Great Britain, Ireland, Italy, Greece, Roumania, the Orange Free State, Bulgaria, Servia, Switzerland, and Belgium, more than three times as large as all Japan, has *four million people,* and only *three mission stations* of the American Presbyterian Church. Yet freedom of worship was sanctioned here ten years ago ; and the Republic in 1872 suppressed all Romish seminaries.

**ECUADOR,** called after the Equator, on which it lies, *has no missionary, and never has had.* Quito, its capital, the highest city in the world, with its 30,000 souls, Guayaquil, its principal commercial centre, and the whole of its *one to two million people* scattered over an area (157,000 sq. m.) considerably larger than Great Britain and Ireland, are wholly unevangelised as yet, unless ceremonial can save us, and the wafer-god be Divine.

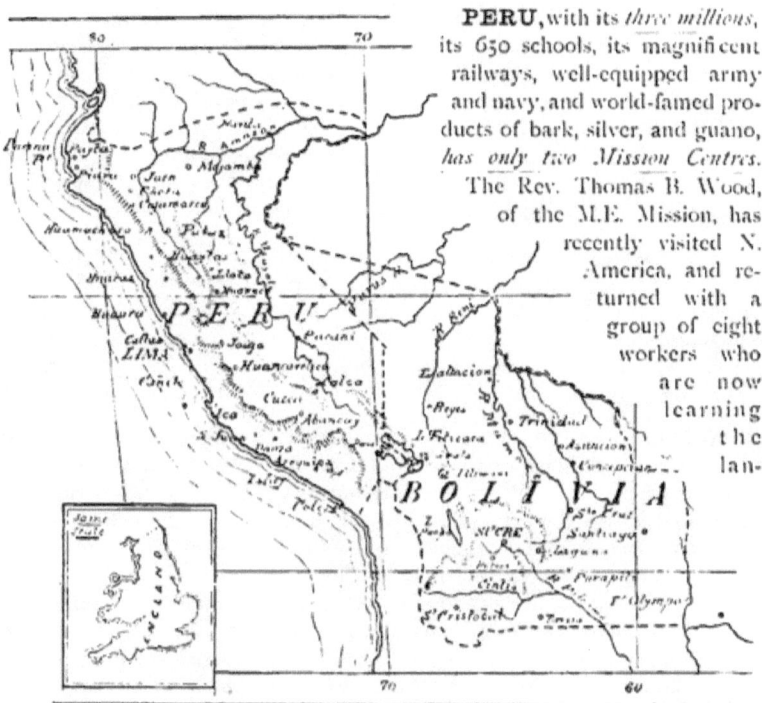

**PERU**, with its *three millions*, its 650 schools, its magnificent railways, well-equipped army and navy, and world-famed products of bark, silver, and guano, *has only two Mission Centres.* The Rev. Thomas B. Wood, of the M.E. Mission, has recently visited N. America, and returned with a group of eight workers who are now learning the lan-

guage, and will shortly be at work, D.V. The American Bible Society and American Methodists, in attempting the evangelisation of Peru, have had a hard struggle with Rome. The priests secured the imprisonment of Signor Penzotti, and have used every means to hinder the preaching of the Word ;

but, as in the other republics, the trend of the times is against them, the tide of civil and religious liberty is rising. After a long fight Signor Penzotti was set free, and there is probably more opportunity for evangelisation to-day in Peru than there ever has been before. A group of itinerant native agents of the American Bible Society are helping to spread the Scriptures, and the little Protestant Churches at Lima and Callao are doing what they can; but taken as a whole the three millions of Peru are to-day still in darkness, waiting for the LIGHT OF LIFE.

**BOLIVIA**, an enormous inland State (area, 567,360 sq. m.), modelled like all the South American Republics on the constitution of the U.S.A., with its President elected every four years, its Congress, universal suffrage and *a population of* 1,450,000, has received one or two passing visits from colporteurs of the noble American Bible Society, but *has no resident Protestant missionary*.

**CHILI**, foremost of all the Republics in intelligence and enterprise, asserted her independence of Spain in 1818. Within twelve months she expelled the Papal nuncio, suppressed an attempt of the clergy to incite revolution, carried the triumph of the liberal party through both Houses of Congress, enacted important civil reforms, and declared the complete and final separation of Church and State.

She possesses nearly 13,000 miles of telegraphic lines, a network of railways, and nearly 1,000 elementary schools. The population of her capital, SANTIAGO, numbers about 150,000; that of VALPARAISO (or Vale of Paradise) almost 100,000; while that of the whole Republic is 3,300,000, *including* 500,000 *Indians*. How many messengers of JESUS are seeking the evangelisation of these three millions? Precisely 24 men and 37 women workers; including a group of Bishop Taylor's mission teachers. The American Presbyterians with four stations and thirteen missionaries, and the South American Missionary Society with three stations, worked by two chaplains, one layman, and some ladies, are labouring (with a group of native helpers) in this long and lovely western coast-land, whose climate is one of the finest in the world, and whose recent political advances make her people especially open to evangelisation—in all perhaps 61. *to reach* 3,300,000!

The **ARGENTINE** and **PATAGONIA**—now reckoned one Republic —form the second largest State in South America, and contain a population of *over four millions.* Closely connected with Europe by steam, the Argentine is also linked by the new transcontinental railway with Chili and the western seaboard. Thousands of Europeans have settled on its prairie ranches, but the bulk of the population is Indian and half-caste, three out of the four millions being non-European. Missionary work here, except in the few cities, is necessarily an itinerant effort among small, scattered centres. Can the four stations and nine workers of the South American Missionary Society, a few independent and Salvation Army workers, and the three stations of the Methodist Episcopal Church of the States, be *enough* to reach these four millions? The question is its own rebuke.

**PARAGUAY**, a little landlocked Republic sandwiched in between the Argentine and Brazil, after labouring under Jesuit government for 200 years, rose in 1811 and asserted her independence of Spain. With an area of 98,000 square miles, about the same size as Great Britain, her population, decimated by recent wars, now only numbers 400,000, of whom 140,000 are largely uncivilised Indian tribes. The South American Missionary Society, with one station and five workers, and the American Methodist Episcopal Church, with a group of native helpers, are working here—*an average of one foreign missionary to 80,000 people !*

**URUGUAY**, the smallest of the South American States (area, 72,110 sq. m., more than twice as large as Ireland), has *a population of 750,000 and but two mission stations* (Methodist Episcopal and South American Missionary Society)—*one to 375,000 souls.*

**BRAZIL**—which alone is larger than the whole United States (area, 3,209,878 sq. m., 270,878 more than U.S.A.[1]), and more than three times exceeds all British India, occupying nearly half the area of South America—has *sixteen million people*, and, as far as we can learn from the Reports of the eight American Societies there working, *not more than one missionary on an average to every* 138,000 *souls.* About a dozen British Christian workers, several of them self-supporting,—among them nine connected with the late Dr. Kalley's Churches in Rio and Pernambuco, and Mr. H. Maxwell Wright, whose devoted itinerant evangelistic efforts are well known—are doing what they can for Brazil ;[2] but, as a glance at our map on p. 68 will show, if a semicircle be described from the town of Sao Paulo as a centre, with a radius of 200 miles, the area included would contain all the mission stations, besides those on the oast-line of this vast Republic. *Of its 16,000,000 people, at least 14,000,000 are still entirely unevangelised.*

The annexed diagrams present at a glance the spiritual destitution of SOUTH AMERICA, which, with a population of 37,000,000, has not quite 400 missionaries, including laymen, women workers, and missionaries' wives. Supposing every missionary there were able to intelligibly communicate the GOSPEL to 10,000 persons—a completely impossible number considering the difficulties of the work, and the scattered, often nomadic character of the population—there would still remain 33,000,000 unreached by the message of free salvation.

DIAGRAM NO. I. represents the population of the whole Continent, massing together in the white squares those who on this exaggerated hypothesis *might* be evangelised, and leaving black the millions unilluminated by the LIGHT of the WORLD. If the number each Protestant missionary could

---

[1] Excluding Alaska.

[2] See Mrs. Kalley's pamphlet, *Help for Brazil.* 6d. Religious Tract and Book Society of Scotland : Edinburgh. London : S. W. Partridge & Co.

reach be estimated at 5,000—a high figure—*only half as many would be evangelised.*

What do these dark squares represent?

### SOUTH AMERICA'S SPIRITUAL NEEDS.

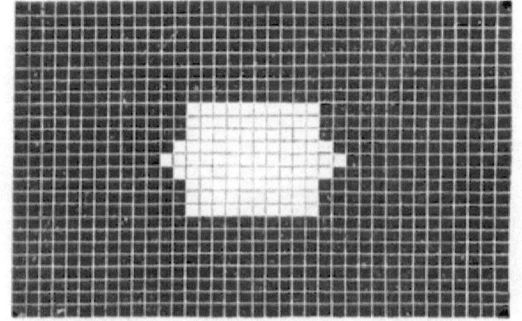

The above diagram (925 squares) represents the population of S. America—37,000,000. Each square = 40,000 persons. If every one of the 400 Missionaries in S. America could reach 10,000 persons, only the central white squares would be evangelised.

Black squares = unevangelised population .. 827 } 925 × 40,000 =
White ,, = partially evangelised popu-
lation ... ... .. 98 } 37,000,000.

DIAGRAM (No. I).

Thirty - three million people under the crushing, deadening influence of Papal policy :—

" ROMANISM," writes Mr. Blackford in his *South American Missions,* " after 300 years of undisputed, uninfluenced power over the education and religion of the Indians, negroes, and amalgamated masses of South America, has left them little better than pagans, with an admixture of Papal forms based in Christianity."

DIAGRAM No. II. is based on the same principle as No. I., but shows the needs of each of South America's great countries (ten Republics, and the three Guianas) separately. The profound spiritual needs of Peru, Bolivia, Ecuador, Colombia, and Venezuela will be seen at a glance.

When will those needs be met?

Swarming priests, friars, and nuns are here, side by side with ignorant masses. Among men a widespread deism, among women cringing super-

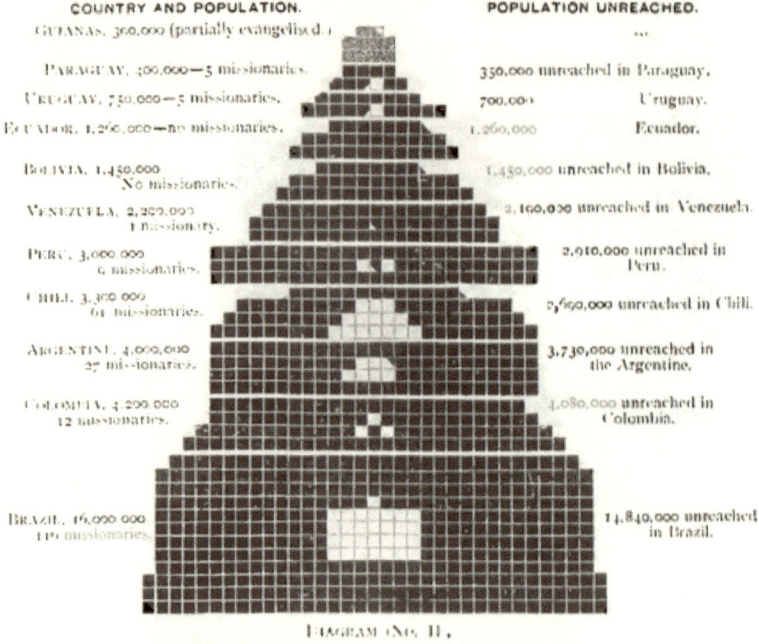

| COUNTRY AND POPULATION. | POPULATION UNREACHED. |
|---|---|
| GUIANAS, 360,000 (partially evangelised.) | ... |
| PARAGUAY, 300,000—5 missionaries. | 350,000 unreached in Paraguay. |
| URUGUAY, 750,000—5 missionaries. | 700,000 Uruguay. |
| ECUADOR, 1,260,000—no missionaries. | 1,260,000 Ecuador. |
| BOLIVIA, 1,450,000 No missionaries. | 1,450,000 unreached in Bolivia. |
| VENEZUELA, 2,200,000 1 missionary. | 2,160,000 unreached in Venezuela. |
| PERU, 3,000,000 6 missionaries. | 2,910,000 unreached in Peru. |
| CHILI, 3,300,000 61 missionaries. | 2,690,000 unreached in Chili. |
| ARGENTINE, 4,000,000 27 missionaries. | 3,730,000 unreached in the Argentine. |
| COLOMBIA, 4,200,000 12 missionaries. | 4,080,000 unreached in Colombia. |
| BRAZIL, 16,000,000 110 missionaries. | 14,840,000 unreached in Brazil. |

DIAGRAM (No. II.)

**DIAGRAM SHOWING THE COMPARATIVE SPIRITUAL NEEDS OF THE TEN REPUBLICS OF SOUTH AMERICA,**

Reckoning that each Missionary could evangelise 10,000 persons

stition, and in both sexes a low standard of morality is everywhere prevalent.

Those who conform to the Church's teaching manifest "an utter absence of spiritual life, and a resting only in outward ceremonials for an inward preparation for the life to come. The apathy and infidel tendencies of the people are due largely to the character of the national Church, and its dissolute priesthood. . . . The people are tired of Papal dominion, and in several of the free Republics the Government casts its influence and moral support on the side of Protestantism."

For what is there in the sterile forms of apostate Christianity to satisfy souls formed in the image of GOD and for companionship with HIM?

Rightly wrote St. Augustine, "Thou hast made us for Thyself, and the heart never resteth till it findeth rest in THEE."

I

## CHAPTER II

### THE NEGLECTED CONTINENT SEALED FOR GOD.

"Such as these have lived and died." LONGFELLOW.

WHEN, IN THE 16TH CENTURY, GOD opened a new world to the sphere of civilization by adding to old Europe the two Americas, His Providence gave the North to Anglo-Saxon Protestantism, and the South to the Papal See. A wind bearing south-west, and a flight of paroquets, diverted Columbus from the northern mainland to the Bahamas, and later to the mouth of the Orinoco, and a similar Divine interposition swept the caravel of Vespucci to Paria and Brazil, leaving North America to be discovered by the vassals of the English kings, while the South came under the sway of Papal crowns.

Yet South America, too, was touched by Puritan faith.

In 1555 three small vessels sailed into the Bay of Rio. They were under the command of Nicholas Durand de Villegagnon, one of the most remarkable, gifted, and unscrupulous men of the 16th century. On board they carried the Pilgrim Fathers of South America, a group of persecuted French Huguenots, sent hither by the good Christian Admiral Coligny.

Upon an island, now overlooked by the capital of Brazil, they landed, after a long and perilous voyage.

"It was upon this island," writes a traveller, "that they erected the first place of worship, and here these French Puritans offered their prayers and sang their hymns of praise nearly threescore years and ten before a pilgrim placed his foot on Plymouth Rock, and more than half a century before the Book of Common Prayer was borne to the banks of the James River."

From this island, and from the pen of the crafty Villegagnon, came the first appeal for Protestant Missions in South America.

'There could be no better haven of rest than this for the persecuted believers,' came the message. 'Send us more colonists. Send us specially a supply of godly ministers from Geneva to spread the doctrines of the Reformed Church in the New World.'

It was a sad, dark story, one of the saddest that the page of history knows. Coligny and Calvin, Farel and Theodor de Beza, who were still watching over the spread of the Reformed doctrines in Europe, responded gladly to the appeal. A party of twelve students, led by two experienced divines, were deputed and sent out forthwith. Journeying through France their number was augmented by persecuted and proscribed Protestant brethren, rejoicing in the prospect of an asylum in the New World, and "freedom to worship GOD." They fought their way through the Papist mob to their three ships at Harfleur, fought their way through wind and storm across the wild Atlantic, and on making the longed-for haven of Rio, had to fight with Portuguese Papists before they could reach their country-men's sea-girt refuge. Hard work at constructing a fort for Villegagnon, with hard fare and little of it, welcomed the colonists. Spiritual scope there was none. Utterly ignorant of the native language, and without opportunities of learning, they found themselves before long in a far worse condition than that from which they had fled. "Villegagnon proved a mere time-serving adventurer, who had probably only affected conformity with the reformed religion for the sake of Coligny's aid and influence in carrying out his colonising scheme. He began by persecuting the Protestants, and finally drove them out of the fort into the open country."

Helpless and unprovided for, the ministers and their flock might still have found a home in, and left lasting blessing to, South America ; but the fair land on whose inhospitable shores they were cast adrift was destined to be the theatre of other than Huguenot history. The Pilgrim Fathers of the South found here no resting-place.

"Villegagnon, after severe and cruel persecution, ultimately allowed the Protestants to return to France ; but he also sent a sealed packet of letters by the captain. One of these was a formal process against the returned colonists, with orders to the magistrates of the ports they should land at to *burn them all as heretics.*

"Storm and disaster attended their homeward passage. The ship leaked so much that constant labour was required to keep it from sinking. They were not many leagues from the shore when provisions ran short, and several of the company had to be landed at the nearest point. Amongst these were three of the Geneva missionaries, Bourdon, Bordel, and Verneuil, two of whom, by Villegagnon's orders, were subsequently thrown into the sea and drowned.

"Meanwhile the leaky vessel, only kept from going to the bottom by incessant pumping, was driven about by storms for weeks together. The carpenter, by constant skilful repairs, saved her, once having to stem the water by treading his coat into a hole whilst he prepared a board to cover the aperture. Another time some powder caught fire, and four men (as well as sails and cordage) were burnt ; one of the sufferers died a few days afterwards.

"As month after month of the long voyage passed by, it became evident that they were all in real danger of death by famine. The monkeys and parrots they were taking home as curiosities were soon disposed of. They were glad to eat a black bitter pottage made of the very sweepings of the store-room, and containing more dirt than food. The rats and mice, themselves enfeebled by famine, were easily caught and devoured. The coverings of their trunks, the leather of their shoes, and even the horn of the ship's lanthorn were eaten. At last there was nothing left but Brazil-wood, one of the driest of all woods. By gnawing this they strove to stay the pangs of hunger.

"'Alas ! my friend,' said Peter Corguilleray to his companion Levy, as they were struggling with the hard Brazilwood, ' I have 4,000 lires due to me in France ; yet I would gladly give a discharge for the whole for a glass of wine and a pennyworth of bread !'"

"Near them lay Peter Richer in his little berth, so prostrate with weakness that he could not raise his head, and constantly engaged in prayer.

"Five or six died of starvation before the five months' voyage ended, and they sighted the coast of Brittany just as the captain had decided to kill a passenger for food on the following day. They landed near Hennebont, and were tenderly cared for by the inhabitants, who commiserated their sad sufferings. The magistrates of the place were favourable to the Reformed faith; they treated Villegagnon's process with contempt, and kindly helped the refugees to return to their homes."[1]

So, amid storm and starvation, fire, suffering, sickness, and death, ended the first attempt to carry the Gospel of JESUS to South America.

[1] *Conquests of the Cross.* Edwin Hodder. Vol. iii. p.98. Cassell. London.

RIO DE JANEIRO.
View of the Harbour and present Town.

"BUSY HOLLAND WITH ITS ACTIVE COMMERCIAL LIFE" (*see page* 87).

Villegagnon's colony failed, and a few years afterwards the Portuguese seized the settlement and reared beside the beautiful bay the city of St. Sebastien, afterwards known as Rio de Janeiro. Its foundations were stained with the innocent blood of the learned John Boles—the last of the French Puritan band, and the first South American martyr. He had fled from Villegagnon's persecution only to languish for eight years in a Jesuit dungeon, and then to wear the crown of martyrdom, whilst Anchieta, so renowned for his holiness and zeal, stood by and prompted the bungling executioner.

Three hundred years went by. The NORTH of the New World, strong in its New England centre of simple, spiritual faith, fought its way slowly up through the fire of its war for Independence and the agony of its slave struggle, to the commonwealth and freedom of to-day.

But the great SOUTH stayed stagnant. No other Pilgrim Fathers sought Brazil. Villegagnon—"*Le Caïn d'Amérique,*" as he was long called by the Huguenots—had brought the first and last. In 1640 a slight attempt was made by the Dutch, then entering Guiana, to do some mission work among the Indians. Their workers left busy Holland with its active commercial life for isolated Guiana, but they were not destined to succeed. The effort was abortive, and left no lasting good.

The dawn of our century of missions flung illuminating beams of heavenly truth across Africa and Asia, lighting the golden Indies, the Empire of the East, and even the extremity of the Dark Continent; but its spiritual radiance fell short of South America, or touched it only at a few isolated points, and for three long centuries the land lay dark and vacant, unentered by any missionaries save the priests of Rome.

What myriads were born, lived, suffered, loved, and passed through death's dim portals in those 300 years—always unsatisfied, always enslaved by passion, habit, sin—always hungering for a Living Bread and Spiritual Water unknown, unknowable!

What yearning was there over them in the great heart of CHRIST, as under the heavy burden of the Apostasy the land that might have been so rich grew ever more wrong and wretched! Across its vast neglected regions the ancient cry rang out and fell unheeded on Christendom's dull ear—"*Many shepherds have destroyed My vineyard, they have trodden My portion under foot, they have made My pleasant portion a desolate wilderness. They have made it a desolation; it mourneth unto Me, being desolate; the whole land is made desolate, because no man layeth it to heart.*"

Christian in name, but practically Pagan, "destroyed" by those who should have been "shepherds,"—"*She mourneth unto Me,*" GOD whispered, "*and no man layeth it to heart.*"

\*　　　\*　　　\*　　　\*　　　\*

His whisper found an echo in a single sainted soul, when in 1805 HENRY MARTYN, on his way to India, touched at Bahia, in Brazil.

" The ardent young soldier of the Cross landed and ascended to the battery that overlooks the beautiful bay of All Saints. Amidst that charming scenery his heart was burdened, and he sought relief in prayer. There, riding at anchor, was the ship that was to carry him to his distant field of service ; there, close beside him, lay outspread the city of Bahia, or San Salvador, teeming with churches, swarming with priests, but with tokens of unbelief or blind superstition on every side. As he gazed upon the scene he repeated the hymn—

'O'er the gloomy hills of darkness
Look, my soul, be still and gaze.'

" Before resuming his voyage, he found opportunities to enter the monasteries, Vulgate in hand, and reason with the priests out of the Scriptures.

" Fascinated by the tropical glories of the coast and interior, and keenly interested in the

" BLIND SUPERSTITION."

Portuguese dons, the Franciscan friars, and the negro slaves—'What happy missionary,' he exclaimed, 'shall be sent to bear the name of CHRIST to these Western regions? When shall this beautiful country be delivered from idolatry and spurious Christianity? Crosses there are in abundance, but when shall the doctrine of the Cross be held up?'.'

It was a memorable picture, second only to the scene 250 years before, when, 1,000 miles farther down the same surf-worn coast-line, the last of the Huguenot pilgrims laid down his life for JESUS and the Gospel. The glowing zeal of Martyn and his prevailing prayers, lighting for so few days on the outskirts of this neglected New World, seem to incarnate the love and thoughts and purposes of GOD for Bahia, Brazil, and the whole Continent his soul embraced. Did they not seal these, even these, as CHRIST's inheritance?

    \*       \*       \*       \*       \*

If the blood of the martyred Rio Huguenots, and Martyn's prayer at Bahia, hallowed central South America to GOD, and pledged to it a place in "the Kingdom that cometh," its lonely frozen Southlands and its tropic North were consecrated by as true devotion, as exalted faith.

Amid ice, snow, and storm; in small boats—unseaworthy, heavy-laden, crowded; adrift among the awful rocks of Tierra del Fuego; beaten by savage Indians from the inhospitable shore in the long nights of the rigorous black winter; forced by ferocious hurricanes to shelter in dank caverns; their scant stock of provisions swiftly lessening day by day; their hopes of relief from Europe fast failing; life itself quickly ebbing away—Allen Gardiner and his six brave companions, pioneers of the Patagonian Mission, bore in their bodies the death-brand of the LORD JESUS CHRIST. Robbed and plundered by the natives; starving on mussels, limpets, and sea-fowl sometimes with difficulty caught; their fish-nets carried off by ice-floes, their guns and powder lost, even their cavern refuges invaded by raging tides, terrific high seas threatening to drown them,—they clung to life for nine awful months, from January to September, 1851.

But their faith in GOD seems never for a moment to have wavered. Famished and perishing, their hearts still overflowed with "mutual affection and jubilant trust in the FATHER for life or for death."

"Asleep or awake," wrote Williams, "I am happy beyond the poor compass of language to tell!"

"Should we languish and die here," wrote Gardiner on his birthday, when the winter (June) snow lay around, "I beseech Thee, O LORD, to raise up others and send forth labourers into Thine harvest!"

His journals are radiant with sunshine of peace and joy in GOD.

Scurvy broke out among them, and, with their other sufferings, helped to hasten the end.

Badcock, one of the strong-hearted Cornishmen, died first.

The failing strength of his comrades was devoted to digging his grave. . . . Six weeks more of hunger and patient waiting for rescue or death, and Erwin expired. Then followed Bryant, both buried by the heroic Maidment.

CAPTAIN ALLEN GARDINER.

A white tablecloth had been hoisted on a prominent tree as a signal to any passing ship, but no sail appeared. On the 29th of August Gardiner wrote farewell letters to his wife and daughters.

"He has kept me in perfect peace. . . . I trust poor Fuegia will not be abandoned If I have a wish for the good of my fellow-men, it is that the Tierra del Fuego Mission might be prosecuted with vigour."

He drafted an "*Outline of a Plan for Conducting the Mission,*" and an "*Appeal to British Christians.*" He wrote in pencil a letter to Williams, destined never to reach him : —

"I tasted nothing yesterday. Blessed be my Heavenly Father for the many mercies which I enjoy—no pain, nor even cravings of hunger, though scarcely able to turn on my bed."

Two days later he wrote what proved to be the last entry in his diary :—" Great and marvellous are the loving-kindnesses of my gracious GOD unto me. He has preserved me hitherto, although without bodily food for three days, yet without any feeling of hunger or thirst."

One more letter, September 6th, 1851, ending, "marvellous loving-kindness to me, a sinner," and then the story was done.

Twenty days after, the *John Davidson*, under Captain Smyley, sent on a special voyage of relief, ran into Banner Cove.

There, within the boat, lay one dead, no doubt Williams ; another on the beach, and another buried. "The sight was awful in the extreme," he wrote. "The two captains who went with me in the boats cried like children. Books, papers, medicine, clothing, and tools were strewed along the beach and on the boat's deck and cuddy." But the gale blew so hard that it gave them barely time to bury the dead and get on board.

Three months later H.M.S. *Dido* touched at the same point, and Captain Morshead found John Maidment in the cavern, and brave Allen Gardiner's body lying beside his boat, where, apparently failing to climb into it, he had fallen and expired. On one of the papers found were written these words, undated :—"If you will walk along the beach for a mile and a half, you will find us in the other boat hauled up in the mouth of a river at the head of the harbour on the south side. Delay not : we are starving."

Rescue had come, but too late !

Thus was the life-seed sown. Thus by martyr-blood was South America's farthest extremity and lowest race sealed too as CHRIST's possession.

The rest of the story it is not ours to tell. Surely every Christian knows its outline : how the tragic news stirred England, how men and means were sent to recommence the lone Fuegia Mission—the struggle to gain a footing among the inhuman, sanguinary Fuegians—the massacre of the first party.

done to death on the open sea-shore—the sixteen martyrs—and the martyrs'
crown when even desolate Fuegia was gathered into the fold of God.[1]

*　　　*　　　*　　　*　　　*

Not only by the Huguenots of Rio, whose tombs in the trackless Atlantic
and scene of martyrdom overlooking the beautiful bay of All Saints,
are among GOD's South American forget-me-nots,—not only by the
prayers of Henry Martyn,—not only by the graves on the sombre Fuegian
shores, has this great Continent been sealed as part of "the kingdom that
cometh." "*Dead man's land*" in Dutch Guiana,—whose climate is even worse
than that of Panama, every foot of whose railway cost a human life to lay,—
glories in a spiritual line connecting this time-scene with the Eternal, laid at
an even greater cost.

The Moravians went there knowing no worse climate existed. They
went there to preach JESUS. But before they could preach they died. Three
or four would arrive together, and in a very short time every one of the
pioneer party be gone. In the first fifty years there were more deaths than
converts. Every soul saved cost a missionary's life.

To-day, in Dutch Guiana, they tell us there is probably more blessing
than in any other mission field. Paramaribo has 14,000 converts out of
22,000—two-thirds of the whole population. The four large Protestant
churches are crowded every week long before the hour of service, overflow
meetings being held for those who cannot contrive to get a hearing through
the open windows crammed with listeners. The largest of these churches is the
spiritual home of a congregation numbering upwards of 8,000, of whom 3,500
are communicants. At Kwathaheda, a district in the heart of Bushland, a
few years ago indescribably foul and heathen, there was not, when a recent

---

[1] "I could not have believed that all the missionaries in the world could have made the
Fuegians honest," wrote Charles Darwin. "The success of the Tierra del Fuego Mission is
most wonderful, and shames me, as I always prophesied utter failure."

mail left, a single idol or idol-house left, *and only two persons remained unbaptized.* The Guianas will be noticed on page 68, shaded grey, instead of black,—they can no more be counted a foreign mission field.

*     *     *     *     *

And was not CHRIST'S seal printed on Peru and the Western Republics in the sufferings, there, of His saints? Penzotti, only a few months since, was dungeon-bound, shut with from 80 to 100 criminals of all descriptions, from common thieves to murderers, month after month, in a half-subterranean jail at Callao, under circumstances that almost parallel Siberian prison life, simply for preaching and distributing the Bible.

> "He is of martyr-stuff," wrote one of his fellow-workers, "and I verily believe would not flinch though the iron stake stood still in the old plaza of the Inquisition at Lima, and the swift-flowing Rimac were ready to bear his ashes to the sea. His people too stand firm, and themselves maintain the meetings with all regularity, while their beloved pastor prays with them in the spirit, from his prison cell. They are fighting, and know they are fighting, the battle of religious liberty for Peru, and GOD will give them the victory."

*     *     *     *     *

"Such as these have lived and died." Such as these have, we repeat it, sealed South America from shore to shore, as part of the inheritance of CHRIST.

"The blood of John Boles and his faithful fellow-servants, who were there slain for the testimony of JESUS, has been crying to GOD for over three hundred years; crying, not for vengeance on their persecutors, but for mercy to their descendants. And that cry comes still to-day to all who by the grace of GOD have obtained like precious faith, beseeching them to carry the light of the GOSPEL to that beautiful land, over which the darkness of Romanism hangs like the shadow of death. Would to GOD a double portion of these lonely martyrs' spirit might fall on many who call themselves servants of the same LORD!"

# CHAPTER III.

## "NO MAN LAYETH IT TO HEART."

"Many shepherds have destroyed My vineyard, they have trodden My portion under foot, they have made My pleasant portion a desolate wilderness. They have made it a desolation: it mourneth unto Me, being desolate; the whole land is made desolate, because no man layeth it to heart."—JER. xii. 10, 11.

SEALED to God; but not—oh, not possessed by JESUS! Martyr-memories irradiate the spots we have just thought of, but between them, still in darkness, lies a Continent as neglected as any other under heaven. Japan is a needy mission field, India's appeal is urgent, and Africa deserves her title "Dark"; but SOUTH AMERICA, from the spiritual standpoint, is as destitute as these.

Imagine an empire extending from England to India, and from the North Cape to Khartoum, scatter across it 37,000,000 people, plunge them for the most part in practical paganism, and then with 400 workers—clerics, laymen, women—"preach the Gospel to every creature" there.

Can this be done?

*Impossible!*

*And can it be the will of God that no more than this be attempted ?*

Has He no care for these millions?　Does He not say their "mourning" comes up before His throne?

The needs of South America exceed not only those of our home lands, but also those of Turkey, Persia, Madagascar, Burmah, and Oceania.

Were the *people to be reached* equally divided among the *preachers*, every minister in Great Britain and the United States would have a parish of 800, in Madagascar of 30,700, in Burmah of 61,000, while in South America he would be responsible for no less than 92,500 souls!

But look at the comparison from another standpoint.　Consider the insufficiency of South America's spiritual supply to her demand.　For her 37 millions she has only 400 workers, including ordained and unordained men, missionaries' wives, men and women teachers, and lady helpers.　For our 37 millions at home we have 60 times as many Church of England clergymen alone; 10 times as many Presbyterian ministers; 4 times as many Baptists; 6 times as many Congregationalists; and 13 times as many Wesleyans. Our Ragged School Union alone numbers 50 times as many teachers as South America has Christian workers of any sort; our Sunday School Union 1,700 times as many.　The officers of the Salvation Army at home outnumber the mission staff of South America 10 times; the British secretaries of the Christian Endeavour Movement three and a half times.　Not to mention our numerous separate and independent home missions—to railwaymen, postmen, policemen, soldiers, sailors, telegraph boys, factory girls, city women, theatrical employés, strolling players and showmen, gipsies, children at the seaside, Jews, foreigners, and even sandwich men, *our Y.M. and Y.W.C.A.'s alone have five times as many secretaries as this neglected continent has Protestant workers of any and every sort.*

Think of the needs of London.　They are great, are they not?　Yet, were you to blot out every Church of England and every Nonconformist chapel, every mission hall and Salvation Army barracks there; to deprive the vast metropolis of every clergyman and lay worker, every Sunday-school teacher, open-air preacher, tract distributor, Y.M. and Y.W.C.A. Secretary,

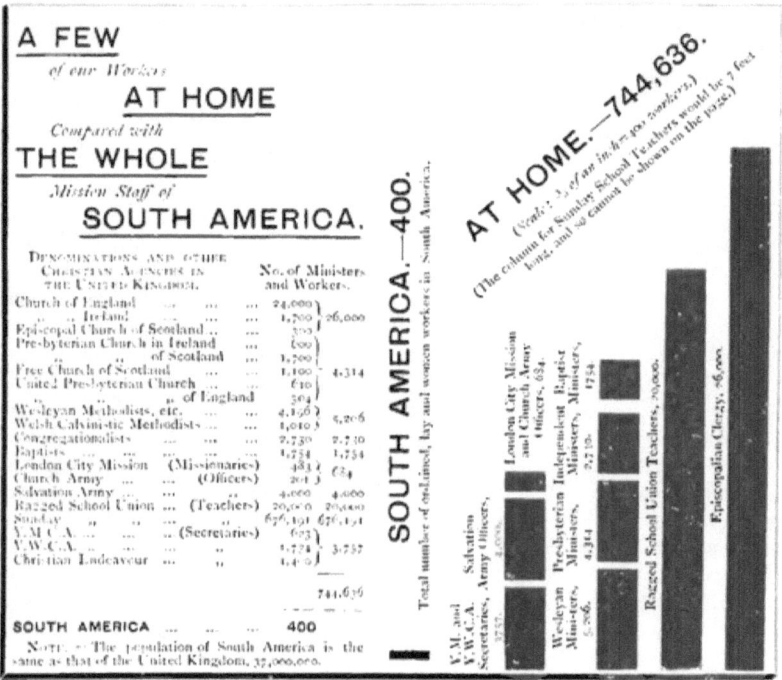

Bible woman, and district visitor; if you were at a single sweep to do away with our thousands of unofficial volunteer helpers and evangelists, leaving

only the London City Mission, you *would still have one hundred more agents at work in London than there are to-day in the whole of South America.*

The annexed diagram speaks for itself.

Such is the need. To meet it what is being done?

### WHAT ARE THE CHURCHES DOING FOR SOUTH AMERICA?

We have not space to dwell on the noble efforts made by the American Churches especially, since in 1836 the Episcopal Methodists sent out their pioneers into the darkness of the Neglected Continent. To the Moravian Church belongs the honour of having led the van a century before, but they never took up work outside Guiana. To-day the American Presbyterians with 20 stations, the American Methodists with 11, and the South American Missionary Society with 16 stations, 22 out-stations, 25 men and 14 women Missionaries, are the largest Protestant agencies at work, while both the English and American Bible Societies stand high.

" *High* . . ." Alas! is it not hard to do this among South American missions. For out of the *265 Missionary Societies at work in the world, only 16 are attempting anything in the Neglected Continent.*

The CHURCH MISSIONARY SOCIETY, with over 736 workers in a dozen different lands, is doing *nothing for South America.*

The BAPTISTS of Great Britain, with 6,205 churches, 1754 pastors, and over 300,000 members, *have not sent a single worker there.*

The CONGREGATIONALISTS of Great Britain and America, with over 7,500 ministers and missionaries, and more than 850,000 communicants, are represented in South America by *one solitary man in Demerara*—an agent of the L.M.S.

The PRESBYTERIAN CHURCH OF ENGLAND, with 11 presbyteries, 290 congregations, and 304 ministers, spends annually over £28,000 on Foreign Missions, but *gives nothing to South America, and maintains no missionary there.*

G

The CHURCH OF SCOTLAND, with its 1,700 churches, 1,700 ministers and licentiates, 604.984 communicants, over 20,000 Sabbath-school teachers, and 2,000 Sabbath schools, raises more than £440.800 a year. It maintains Zenana agents, schools, missionaries, and teachers abroad, but *ignores entirely the existence of the people of this vast Continent, devoting to them neither men nor means.*

The FREE CHURCH OF SCOTLAND, with its more than 1,047 churches. 1,100 ministers, and a membership of 343,015, holds an honourable place among the Churches for its devotion to the Foreign Mission cause. Its labourers are working in India, South Africa, Syria, the West Indies, Arabia, the New Hebrides, and among the Jews, but *no missionaries have gone from the Free Church to South America yet.*

The UNITED PRESBYTERIAN CHURCH, with 610 ministers, over 187,075 members, 7 mission presbyteries, a foreign membership of 16,500, and an income of nearly £400,000 per annum, is *not doing, and never has done, any missionary work in South America.*

The METHODISTS of Great Britain and Ireland, with over 5,206 ministers, and over one million members, are famed for their world-wide foreign missions, whose active organization forms into " district " Churches the wide outlying regions of Colonial and even heathen fields. But the Methodists of Great Britain *have not a single missionary or a single circuit in South America.*

Among the Methodists we include the BIBLE CHRISTIANS, WESLEYAN METHODISTS, METHODIST NEW CONNECTION, PRIMITIVE METHODISTS, WESLEYAN REFORM UNION, INDEPENDENT METHODISTS, and the UNITED METHODIST FREE CHURCHES.[1]

The FRIENDS, who in 1891 numbered in Great Britain 340 meetings and over 16,000 members, have not a few missionaries, but *none here.*

---

[1] British Wesleyans at one time reached Guiana, and the Wesleyan W. Indian Conference, which maintains a mission manned by 9 men there, still receives a diminishing annual grant from the Parent Society.

The AMERICAN BAPTIST MISSIONARY UNION, which has over 1,100 stations, 129 missionaries, and over 68,000 communicants in the foreign field, has *never attempted anything for South America*.

To put the state of the case in diagrammatic form:—if the 265 Missionary Societies labouring for the evangelization of heathendom, and the 16 at work for South America, be represented by a square apiece, the contrast is as below:—

**265 Societies at work for all the World.**

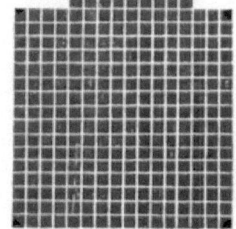

**16 Societies working for South America.**

NOTE.—One of these Societies—the L.M.S. —maintains only 1 man in the field; another only 7 workers, and two others only 5.

But the real state of the case is much worse than this— the Neglected Continent, far more neglected. For in the comparative proportion of *workers* there is, as shown by the annexed two columns, a still greater gap.

The four following chapters (each of which is complete in itself, and independent of the rest of this brief sketch) summarise, from a missionary standpoint, the past story and present state of ARGENTINA, BRAZIL, the REPUBLICS of the WEST, and the ABORIGINES of South America.

Column representing the whole No. of foreign missionaries in the world.

Column representing the whole No. of missionaries in South America.

# CHAPTER IV.

## CAN THE WORK BE DONE? A PRACTICAL ANSWER FROM THE ARGENTINE.

*"He who is not ready to preach the Gospel anywhere, is fit to preach it nowhere."*

ONE Saturday afternoon, fifteen years ago, a young south-country man entered the village schoolhouse of Bishops Wood. The place was empty as usual at this time of the week. John H. L. Ewen had expected to find it so. He came here weekly at this hour for quiet thought and prayer. Twenty-four years of age, he had been led, twelve months before, under a deep sense of spiritual realities, to consecrate his life to GOD, and was already known as a village preacher.

The sun was low to-day as he crossed the threshold, and, for the first time, a map hanging on the schoolhouse wall, and lit by the glow of afternoon, caught his attention. It was a map of South America. He crossed to look at it, mechanically tracing the long coast-line from tropical Trinidad to frozen Fuegia, and the storm-beaten shores of Cape Horn, the great mountain backbone of the Andes, and the open plains of the Argentine. He noted the sea-board cities, and as he stood there, felt the birth of a new thought within him—a question that answered itself.

"What do the people who live in these cities know of GOD? How many along these rivers, how many in these inland plains, are to-day without CHRIST? What do they *believe* in South America?"

Presently he knelt down by the map.

"Oh, my GOD," he prayed, "why should these multitudes be left without the knowledge of Thy love, without JESUS CHRIST and eternal life through Him, while we have so much light?"

Time passed while he knelt in the silence. Then a new prayer rose in his heart:—

"If it be Thy will, send me to preach CHRIST in South America."

Years afterwards a tall theological student was walking down Bow Road with Dr. Grattan Guinness, Director of the East London Institute for Home and Foreign Missions.[1]

"I feel, sir," the young man was saying, as they threaded their way through the crowded thoroughfare, "that I cannot remain another session at the Institute. I must get into the work. I long to make known the good news of Salvation to those who have never heard."

"What part of the mission field is on your mind?"

"The same I mentioned to you when I entered the Institute — South America."

MR. J. H. L. EWEN.

With a look of surprise the older man drew a letter from his pocket, saying, "I have just received this from

---

a gentleman there, telling me that if any one felt led to go out, he would be glad to give him a home for the time being."

It was another link in the chain of guidance that was leading J. L. Ewen out to the Neglected Continent.

A few months later he found himself on South American shores. And as perhaps no better answer can be found to the question, "How may the work be done in South America?" than a story of work accomplished, we subjoin some extracts from his unpublished account of evangelisation in the Argentine.

One of the first Spaniards I met in Buenos Ayres, though the son of a Christian mother, was himself an ungodly young man. He avoided any one who was at all likely to speak to him about his soul. Alas, there were very few he needed to avoid !

He was anxious to learn English, and kept with me, as I knew nothing of Spanish. One day, in the garden, I repeated to him in Spanish a verse of Scripture, which I had learnt for the purpose. My pronunciation was so incorrect that I feared he might not have understood, and also that, if he had, it might make him try to avoid me. A few days afterwards I left the city. Three weeks later, when passing again through Buenos Ayres, a friend accosted me with—

"You will be glad to hear that Miguel C—— is converted. His mother tells me it is through what you said to him in the garden."

How I praised God for this first-fruit ! Miguel began to work for CHRIST at once, and later on took charge of the Evangelical School. He spoke in public in a bright, attractive way, and many gathered round to listen to his earnest words, which were owned and blessed of GOD. After five years of useful Christian life, a sharp and swift attack of cholera cut short his work down here.

Never shall I forget his last words to me. I was going home on furlough, and he had come down to see me off.

"Brother Ewen," he said as we paced the landing-stage together, "tell me, are there *no* Christians in England ?"

"Yes," I answered, "hundreds of thousands."

"Then," he sadly said, "why do they not come out here ? You have only to announce a meeting in any street of Buenos Ayres, and people will crowd in till there is not standing room. *But who is there to preach ?*"

\*   \*   \*

Thousands of English-speaking settlers are scattered over *El Campo* ("the camp" or country) of the Argentine. Many, during long years of sheep and cattle farming, have never been visited by a missionary, though they welcome with hearty hospitality any one seeking their spiritual welfare. Good work might be done by earnest, godly, and physically capable young men, willing to horse is tied if the owner of the hut be at home, indicates human habitation. For the rest, brilliant sunshine everywhere, cloudless blue overhead, and endless undulating pampas, varied here and there by occa-

"LONG YEARS OF SHEEP AND CATTLE FARMING."

rough it, going from place to place, not knowing where their night's rest may be found.

*El Campo* is a great plain. As far as eye can see, nothing is visible but tall pampas grass waving before the wind, like the rolling of the ocean. No hills or woods break the monotony. Here and there a mud hut thatched with pampas, with a corral or sheep-enclosure, and a post to which a sional *estancias* and by forests of thistles, five to ten feet high, through which the traveller must push as best he can—complete the scene.

Compass in hand, and with a thick stick as my only companion, I set out for the nearest rancho, on my first evangelistic tour. An hour's walk and I reached a hut. Its owner, a tall, honest-faced *Gaucho*, could only speak Spanish. It was useless to attempt conversation, and bowing my thanks for his polite fluency, I left. Half an hour later the second hut was reached, in the shade of which were lying three evil-looking men. I had been repeatedly warned, before leaving the city, not to venture out alone. Crossing the lonely *campo* one is often far from safe. One morning, some ranchers, looking at their pistols, inquired what kind of one I used?

" I do not carry a pistol or a revolver," I replied.

" What, travelling about as you are, Mr. Ewen, with no pistol! Don't you carry a knife ? "

" No, but I carry a small sword," said I, taking my Bible from my pocket.

" Well, I wouldn't go a hundred yards from the house without my pistol," exclaimed one of the young men, " I should think it imprudent to do so."

To-day it really seemed that I had fallen in with dangerous companions. To have turned back would have been to show my fear, so I kept on steadily, thanking the GOD who shut the lions' mouths for His presence and keeping power. When almost exhausted with my long walk in the burning sun, a third hut appeared in the far distance. To my joy and relief I soon found that its inhabitants, a father, mother, and half a dozen children, spoke English. It was not much of a home—four mud walls, thatched with pampas grass, divided into two rooms ; but the hearty hospitality, and the cheery kettle put on at once for tea in honour of my visit, made up for all defects.

I gathered the children round me, and with much difficulty endeavoured to teach them John iii. 16.

" Do you *never* speak to your children about GOD ?" I said to the mother.

" Well, sir, what can I do?" she answered. " I came to this country when I was eight years old. What little I knew of the Bible I forgot long ago. I have never since had a chance of going to a place where it is read."

We had reading and prayer together, and when I left, the elder son accompanied me some distance. He was evidently under deep conviction of sin, and when we were alone, poured out his heart to GOD. It was a simple prayer—

" O GOD, JESUS died for sinners, and I am a sinner, and I believe He died for me. Thou hast said, ' He that believeth on Him is saved.' "

Thus, as a little child, he entered the kingdom of heaven.

In the next hut the *estancero* (farmer) was at first most unfriendly, keeping as far as possible from my chair, as though a mad dog sat on it. We had tea, however, and I asked if I might read. He listened with interest, knelt reverently for prayer, and his manner entirely changed.

" If ever you are near us again," he said, when we rose from our knees, " don't pass without calling. I am sorry I have no room to offer you a night's rest. We will gladly lend you a horse, if you like."

I had neither bridle nor saddle at this

time, and so could not accept this characteristic offer.

The method of inland travel here is, that whoever has shown you hospitality for the night will provide you a horse for to-morrow, if you have your own bridle and saddle. In this way one can travel any distance in the interior on horseback.

At the next place my experience was the same, and as I went on from place to place, trackless plain, some such outline as this would be given :—

"Keep straight on in a south-easterly direction, and when you have travelled for about half an hour you will see a small *monte* just on the horizon ; keep a little to the right, and you will see a larger one, there you will find Mr.———"

Sometimes the sun had set when I started for a journey of over thirty miles, crossing

A RIVER IN THE ARGENTINE.

among people who in many cases had never before heard of GOD's redeeming love in the gift of His SON, it was gratifying in many instances to see strong men bowed down under a sense of sin. Not infrequently those who were watching their cattle wept as they listened to "the old, old story of JESUS and His love."

The directions, from day to day, were somewhat vague. As I set out across the dangerous rivers by moonlight—rivers neither deep nor wide, but with beds so soft that horses sometimes sink and disappear. Often my steed, for the time being, had not been broken in, and gave me a lively time. But difficulties were nothing in view of the results GOD graciously granted. A lad of sixteen, the youngest son of one family, was converted. I left him the same day, never expecting to meet again, but two years later came across him unexpectedly, at a railway station. His happy face and bright testimony proved unmistakably that the good seed had fallen into good ground in his case.

At one far interior *estancia*, where, however, no comfort was lacking, I found the family at dinner. When the ladies left the dining-room, I said, " May I read a chapter, and have what we call in England family worship ?"

" I will ask my wife," replied the host, somewhat confused.

Presently he returned, and said with uncomfortable hesitation, " Will you kindly excuse us refusing ? We are all Roman Catholics."

An awkward silence followed, though I tried to recommence conversation.

" Do you play the piano ?" asked my host.

" Well," I said, " at school long ago, I was able to. If you like, I will try something I know still."

The late Mrs. Denning's tune to *Passing Onward* occurred to me, and I played and sang —

" Passing onward, quickly passing,
   But I ask thee whither bound ?
   Is it to the many mansions
   Where Eternal rest is found ?
   Passing onward, passing onward,
   Tell me, sinner, whither bound ? "

Before the verse was ended, the lady and her visitors came back into the room, and said, " Please go on ; we should like to hear. "

I repeated the hymn, verse by verse, quoting Scriptures, endeavouring to show them the need of present salvation.

The opportunity that followed was a good one.

" Do not think," said the lady at the close, "that any lack of respect to you made us refuse to have family worship ; but the priests have made us promise not to have the Bible read in our house."

The *estancero* would hardly let me get away.

" We cannot let you go," he said, " till you promise that when you come this way again you will stay a few days with us."

On leaving, he gave me his favourite horse and a guide.

I frequently passed *ranchos* where natives lived, who, of course, had never seen the Bible or heard of the " good news." At one station they were suffering from drought.

" Thousands of our sheep will die unless the rain comes soon," remarked a householder.

" GOD is able to give rain," I answered and I prayed with them that He would.

At midnight a thunderstorm came on, and it rained steadily till seven o'clock next day.

They spoke of it as a direct answer to prayer. On Sunday, forty of the settlers gathered. I spoke from Acts xiii. 42. The LORD was with us in power and blessing ; many were weeping, and amongst those whom I hoped received blessing was one of the sons belonging to the house where I prayed for rain.

Part of my journeys were made by rail,

when I used at times to sit on the triangular cow-catcher in front of the engine—a pleasant place, as it is free from dust, but dangerous, as one may be abruptly brought into contact with wild cattle.

Most of the time spent in travelling was occupied in speaking on the all-important subject. Among the officials of the line, I came across one testimony which I cannot but repeat. It was from a young engineer, of whom I had seen enough to know that amid much immorality he was living a stainless life.

"I feel sure," he remarked, "that my being kept in times of temptation when many others have fallen, is due to my mother's early training."

\* \* \*

On returning to Buenos Ayres, I met a young German, to whom, after a pleasant chat in my room, I said, taking up my Bible, "Now tell me, are you a Christian?"

The HOLY SPIRIT was evidently working with him. We had some earnest conversation and prayer. . . .

"If you have time to come in to-morrow night, look me up," I said when he left.

Next day he came with such a happy face. He had found peace and joy in CHRIST, and for him a new life had begun.

A few days afterwards I left again for *El Campo*. When I returned, my German friend had gone.

"O——'s is such a wonderful case of conversion," a friend told me. "Knowing German, English, French, and Spanish, he bears a bright testimony to all around. He is gone now to the interior, 400 miles inland. The young men with whom he works gave a dinner to welcome him among them. After the usual congratulatory speeches had been made, he rose and told the story of his conversion, pleading with them to accept the SAVIOUR who had done so much for him, and gave them each a copy of the New Testament."

Though frequently cheered by cases of blessing, the evangelist's heart could not but be saddened by the greatness of the needs around him, and the limitation of his own life-work.

Late one afternoon (he wrote) I arrived at a station, where I was deeply solemnised on hearing of the recent death of a young unmarried man, the owner of a well-stocked league of land. Poor fellow, he had lain there on his dying bed, no one within hundreds of miles to point him to the SAVIOUR!

At this *estancia* a young man was sleeping, like myself, for the night. He had set his heart on making a fortune, and spoke of nothing but the best means of attaining his object. Not long after he was gored to death when "working cattle." He had only been a few months in South America.

Willingness to listen always marked these lonely settlers, however far they might seem from "the life that is life indeed." After an address at a *caseta* — a little house on wheels used by surveying engineers — a young man came up, saying,—

"I will drive you to the train to-morrow if you will give me the pleasure. You must be tired after travelling on horseback such long distances."

Next morning, accordingly, we drove off together. I was glad of the opportunity of seeing him alone.

"When you were speaking to us all last night," he said, after some conversation, "I was enabled to trust in the finished work of CHRIST."

How one's heart rejoiced at such good news! We parted immediately after, but I left him in the Light.

\*     \*     \*

Travelling in a ballast train to Tandil, I spoke to a young man about spiritual things. He appeared much annoyed. I invited him to the Sunday services, but he only rudely laughed, and tried to discourage my attempts to get the men to come. Later on, however, he entirely changed his opinions, and became my willing helper, inviting all

"WORKING CATTLE" (*see p.* 107).

the *employés*, whom he knew where to find, and gathering a large number to the services.

Thousands of English-speaking people in the Argentine are in great spiritual need, but the Spanish population—in still greater darkness—may be counted by millions. About this time I decided to learn Spanish, in order to reach the natives.

The way for my doing so was opened

through the unexpected kindness of the post-master of Tandil, a small town over 200 miles south of Buenos Ayres. Hearing of my arrival, Don Pedro came down at once.

"You want to learn Spanish?"

will be good for both of us; every spare moment we can speak to each other, and learn."

"I shall be very glad to," I answered; "but before accepting, will you not tell me

ENGLISH AND SPANISH IN THE ARGENTINE.

"Yes," I said, "I do."

"And I want to learn English; so, if you will teach me English, I will teach you Spanish. Are you going into lodgings?"

"Yes, I hope to."

"Come, then, and live at my house. It

how much I may expect to pay for board and lodging?"

"Oh, nothing; certainly not."

"Thank you," I said; "I cannot come on those terms. You must allow me to pay something."

"If you pay me, we are not friends."

"You had better go, and say nothing more about payment," the interpreter broke in ; "you can settle it later on : you see how determined he is."

I went, and with the utmost kindness Don Pedro gave me the best room in his house.

Conditions in the city were very far from safe. One evening, after I had been there a short time, I went out for a walk. In the middle of the road, on my way home, a tall man came quickly towards me, and when abreast of me, turned suddenly in the darkness, came up and drew his knife. I saw the gleaming steel above his head, and expected to be stabbed, but an unseen hand restrained him. Without uttering a word, he turned and fled.

Don Pedro met me at the house door. "I am glad you have arrived safely!" he exclaimed. "There has been a murder at the corner."

The man who had attempted to stab me was the same who had just committed the murder, and was now attempting to escape. This was but one of the many deliverances which the LORD wrought for me.

The kindness of my host could not have been exceeded. That I might learn Spanish more quickly, he gave up studying English at first to prevent confusing the two tongues.

"Don Pedro," I remarked one evening, "I am not happy here."

"Not happy, Mr. Ewen ; what is the matter? what can we do for you?"

"Do for me," I replied : "that is just the trouble ! You do too much for me. I am receiving your hospitality and help, and paying nothing. I shall really have to leave."

"You do not mean to say that that is troubling you !" he exclaimed, with a smile of relief.

"Yes, it is ; and really it must not go on any longer."

"Pastora," he called to his wife, "Mr. Ewen is not happy."

She looked concerned. "What is it?" she inquired. "We will gladly do anything you want."

"Do not be anxious," explained my host ; "the trouble is that he wants to pay us."

Mrs. Borallarros was even more difficult to deal with than her husband.

"We are glad to have you," she said. "Pedro has been better ever since you came. I believe he would die if you left ! Do us the favour, sir, never to speak of this money matter again."

Though I could not promise this, I never succeeded in persuading these generous friends to accept any payment for my stay.

They were Spanish Roman Catholics, and from the first I sought the LORD for their conversion. One night, when Don Pedro came in, I was reading from my Spanish Bible.

"*Que libro es eso?*" he asked. ("What book is that?")

"It is the Bible," I replied.

"What! the Holy Bible?" he said with astonishment. "I have never seen the Holy Bible." Grasping the book eagerly, he opened it at the first chapter of Genesis, reading to himself with the deepest interest chapter after chapter, only breaking the silence by frequently exclaiming, "*Que libro preciosa!*" etc. He read on to the twenty-fifth chapter with unabated interest. When he discovered how late it was, and that he was keeping me up, he closed the Bible, saying, "Well, this is a splendid book!"

"Yes," I answered, "I like the whole of it very much; but there are some parts that seem to me still more interesting." I turned to John iii. 16, saying—

"Read this, Don Pedro."

He saw that it was in the middle of the chapter, and the third chapter, so he turned to the first chapter and read to the fourth, then closing it, said most emphatically,—

"It is a splendid book."

"The first '*rancho*' . . . a miserable-looking place."

We then retired to rest. I was curious to see if he would care to read it the following night, and to my great satisfaction, as soon as he entered the door, he said, "Where is the Bible?"

He continued reading again until a late hour, beginning where he had left off the night before. This went on night after night. I went to Buenos Ayres one day for the express purpose of buying two Spanish hymn-books. Next evening, when Don Pedro had read his chapters, I said,—

"I have a hymn-book here, Don Pedro."

"What is it like?" he asked, turning over the leaves and expressing his delight. "Can you sing this one?"

"I never sang a Spanish hymn in my life, but I will try to put a tune to it."

Having counted the lines and found out the metre, I sang to the tune of "*Come ye sinners, poor and wretched*," endeavouring to keep the Spanish lines and tune running together. Towards the end of the hymn I had gained a little confidence, and was able to look off my book to see how Don Pedro was getting on; and found him with his eyes closed, and his face upturned, singing with heart and soul, —

> "*Jesu Christo angustiado,*
> *Clama a tu mi corazon;*
> *Vida gracia a ti pidiendo,*
> *Y eterna salvacion.*" etc.

My heart leaped for joy, saying, "Surely he is a saved soul." And so it seemed, for a few days after he came running to my room, saying.—

"Mr. Ewen, give me a Testament!"

As soon as he had got it, he ran back to the Post-office again. He had been speaking to a man about his soul's salvation. The man naturally wanted to know where he had learnt what he was saying, so he came for a Testament, and having referred him to many Scriptures, presented him with the book. Many, many times he came to ask for Testaments to give away; and he has the honour of being the first to distribute Scriptures in the town of Tandil.

\*    \*    \*

As soon as I knew enough Spanish, I went out of the town to visit, taking a few copies of the Gospel of St. John. The first *rancho* I found was a miserable place, without chimney or window. From behind a hide swinging over the entrance, a little smoke escaped. Country fashion, I clapped my hands to announce a new arrival. A long-haired, dark-complexioned *Gaucho* appeared.

"*Adalante!*" he said. ("Come in.")

I crept into the dark hut behind the hide. There was not an article of furniture in it, but a number of bullocks' skulls were lying about, to be used as seats. A woman was sitting by the fire.

"Sit down," said my host.

For a moment the weird aspect of the place I had got into drove away my Spanish, and they evidently thought I neither spoke nor understood their tongue. The man passed me some *maté*. [1]

While I drank it the woman remarked in an undertone, "Now is our time to see what he has got."

In a moment I said, "What do you think of this?" repeating John iii. 16, and continued speaking of the love of GOD in the gift of His Son. They seemed awe-stricken. After delivering my message, and giving each of them a Gospel, I got away in safety through the mercy of GOD.

Next time I went I found the *Gaucho* alone; and the following Sunday he was outside with several young men, and evidently did not want me, though his native politeness made him invite me in.

"Shall I read a hymn?" I began; "and shall I sing it to you?"

The proposal pleased him. Very soon the young men came in, one after another, took off their hats, and sat quietly down. They listened most attentively while I read the Scriptures and pointed them to the SAVIOUR. Two of them had just come from dark Bolivia, where up to that time the Bible had never found an entrance, as the Scriptures

---

[1] A kind of Paraguayan tea, extensively used in South America, made of the leaves and green shoots of a species of holly.

were prohibited by the Republic at the in-
stigation of the Romish priests.

Now there is freedom for the Word of
God there, may it run, have free course, and
be glorified.[1]

I have reason to believe that my visits
were blessed to the *Gaucho*. His simplicity
was touching. Poor man, one day, when
very much affected by what I had been
saying, he wanted to give me something as
an expression of his thankfulness, and offered
me five eggs.

*          *          *

I remained in Don Pedro's house for over
a year; and at the end of that time, if there
was any difference in their kindness, it was
that they were kinder at the end than at the
beginning of our acquaintance.

"I am longing for you to be able to preach
the Gospel in Spanish in this town," he
often said: "the people are ready for it."

There was an unused Danish church in
the place: I inquired as to its rent.

"We will place it at your service free of
charge," was the reply: "and many of us
will be glad to attend the meetings."

So the work went on.

At Montevideo, the Methodists requested
me to be their minister, and earnestly sought
to convince me that it was my duty to
accept the call. I could only reply, "As
long as there are millions on the continent
destitute of the Word of God, and knowledge
of JESUS CHRIST, it will be impossible for
me to devote my time and energy to those
who have both."

An answer worth remembering. Were but that conviction more widespread, how many thousands of pastors, teachers, preachers, evangelists,
laymen, and women workers would go out into earth's dark lands, gladly
leaving those who need them, for those who need them most!

Returning by rail (writes Mr. Ewen) to
the Interior, I came across a young Spanish
doctor, to whom I gave a New Testament.

"I am sorry," he remarked, accepting it
gladly, "that I have nothing to give you in
return."

"You will please me most," I answered,
"if you will read the book."

"I shall be glad to read it," he replied.

A month later, we met, apparently by
chance, at the same station. As soon as
the train started, he put his hand into his
pocket, and took out the New Testament,
saying, —

"This book you so kindly gave me I have
read through more than once."

[1] This was written several years ago; but even now, in 1894, Bolivia has no resident missionary, and never has had,
though two or three native agents of the American Bible Society are at work among its two to three million people.

"Have you? I am glad to hear it."

"Yes," he said: "the night I got out to my uncle's *estancia*, when dinner was over (there was a large family of us at the table — about 17), I asked my uncle if I might be allowed to read a little from a book a friend

CEMETERY, CORDOBA, ARGENTINE.

had given me. I began to read from the first chapter, and read several. They were all much pleased, and asked me to read again the next night, beginning where I had left off. I continued every night, reading several chapters at a time, until I have read the book more than once. My uncle wanted

me to give him it; but I told him that as it was a present from a friend, I could not part with it, but if there were any to be had in Buenos Ayres like it, I would be sure to send him one."

I had great pleasure in giving him another to send to his uncle, marking such portions as John iii. 16. I have good hope that the young doctor is a chosen one in CHRIST.

\*      \*      \*

In all my experience in Spanish work, I only met with one refusal of a Gospel tract. Returning from an open-air meeting at Cordoba, I crossed the road to give a tract to a policeman, who was sitting in the shade of a house. A woman with a baby was sitting by him.

"I don't want it," he said.

"I suppose you don't know what it is," I replied; "but I will read a little of it to you."

And I began reading the three verses at the end of the tract, with the Gospel beautifully expressed in Spanish.

When I came to the end of the first verse, the poor woman eagerly stretched out her hand, saying,—

"Sir, I'll have one; *that's what I want for my poor soul.*"

The man listened with deep interest while I read some portions of Scripture, and when I said,—

" Now, tell me, why didn't you want it?" he answered,—

" Because I can't read, sir."

A good reason for not wanting it! This is the only refusal I ever had.

\*    \*    \*

" I took my Bible with me," said a young man who had been attending some of my *estancia* meetings—" I took my Bible with me when I went to see my old father and mother, who live twenty miles away. I told them about trusting only in CHRIST. A neighbour came in and listened. 'What a wonderful book! I never heard anything like it!' she said. 'I should like to get one.'

" I called to see her afterwards. 'Where is your book?' she said. 'Will you sell it me? Do let me have it. I will give you anything for it that you like.'

" How I should rejoice," he concluded, " if I could go from town to town reading and selling the Scriptures!"

Like every new-born soul, he wanted others to share his joy.

\*    \*    \*

Everywhere these people are sitting in darkness and the "shadow of death," living and dying without GOD. The Bible is an unknown book, so unknown that it is no

THE CATHEDRAL, CORDOBA.

uncommon thing to have to explain what it is.

Money and pleasure are enthroned as gods, and rule supreme over the hearts and lives of hundreds of thousands of Spanish, Italian, French, German, and British emigrants, who have been pouring into the country of later years, while the original *Gaucho* settlers have long since thrown off all semblance of religion, and are living for the most part outlawed lives.

Throughout the whole republic, including the great city of Buenos Ayres, greed for money and abandonment to gross sensual pleasure have demoralised all classes. . . . There is no public opinion to repress immorality. . . . Even among business men there is mutual distrust, and the priesthood is so openly immoral, that its sins and follies are exposed to public view in the cartoons of the comic papers.

Yet the country is open to Christian work. The President of the Republic and some members of the Government have at times attended Protestant meetings, expressed favourable opinions of the missionaries' influence, and wished them success. In 1884 the Government passed in our Bible carriage,[1] with its contents, free of duty, the Mayor of Buenos Ayres himself paying our license to sell Bibles. Editors of local papers in almost every town have inserted commendatory notices of the Bible carriage and its work. When I first went out as a missionary to the British settlers, a leading member of the Board of Directors sent me, unsought, a free pass over a thousand miles of the Southern Railway in furtherance of the work. *The door is wide open into the homes and hearts of the people.*

THE PLAZA, BUENOS AYRES.

" The door is open."

Who will enter in?

As long as there are millions destitute of the Word of God and know-

[1] To support the workers, defray the expenses of the carriage, and supply books, costs from £200 to £300 a year. Dr. H. R. Hadden, 68, Grosvenor Road, Rathmines, Dublin, will gladly receive and acknowledge subscriptions, and keep friends informed of the progress of the work. Mr. Ewen's present address is Kendal Cottage, Calle Independencia, Tandil, Argentine Republic, South America.

ledge of JESUS CHRIST, should it not be impossible for us to devote our life-work to those who have both ?

Families living out on " the camp " farms are constantly wanting tutors, as their children cannot go to schools.

" Are there not young Christian men," writes Mr. Torre, of Buenos Ayres, " who would not mind going out into the country at first as tutors, roughing it somewhat, getting a good grip of the language, and then just wait on GOD for future guidance ? There would always be opportunities for witnessing. What they need most to learn before they come out is not Greek, Latin, and logic, so much as to depend alone on GOD for strength and food, communion and fruit-bearing.

" My idea is self-support. Where a man's heart is right, there is generally found a good amount of time to give to definite work for the LORD."

" 'Son, go work to-day in my vineyard. ...
He answered . . . ' I go, sir' : . . . .
and went not."

MATT. xxi. 28-30.

# CHAPTER V.

## THE LAND OF THE HOLY CROSS.

*"What happy missionary shall be sent to bear the name of Christ to these Western regions? When shall this beautiful country be delivered from idolatry and spurious Christianity. Crosses there are in abundance, but when shall the doctrine of the Cross be held up?"*—HENRY MARTYN (written from Brazil).

### Part I. A Page from a Missionary Life.

BY THE REV. S. L. GINSBURGH, OF BRAZIL.

THE names on the visitors' cards were unknown to me, and the gentlemen who brought them, strangers.

"We have come from Amargosa," they explained on entering, "to beg you to visit us and preach to the people the Gospel of the LORD JESUS."

" But who directed you to me ? "

" One of your colporteurs, from whom we bought a Bible and tracts, in Amargosa. We read and re-read the tracts, and were so deeply interested in the Bible, that we longed to know more about it. Your address was printed on one of the tracts, and we resolved to come to you for further enlightenment concerning the wonderful words we read in the book."

Here was a real cry from Macedonia ! Gladly would I have gone and

118

told these people the story of JESUS, but how could I spare time? How leave the Church in Bahia, the printing office, and other important matters? I could only promise to visit them as soon as possible. In about two months the opportunity came.

Amargosa is about 120 miles from the capital of Bahia. One has to cross the bay, and travel six or seven hours up a winding, shallow river, and to disembark and wait till the following morning for the train which leaves at 6 a.m. and arrives about mid-day.

It is an important commercial centre. Thousands come to its weekly fair to sell their tobacco, coffee, farinha, etc. It has many beautiful shops, some of them richly decorated, equal to those of Rio and Bahia. The population is only 3,000, but is increasing rapidly. Signs of progress are seen everywhere. It has two journals, one weekly and one fortnightly; two public schools and three private ones. French science and art are taught. Its railroad was inaugurated two months ago. Its one Roman Catholic Church is old and dilapidated. I found the city crowded, it being market day, with hundreds of people on mules, on horseback, and on foot—whites, blacks, and real red Indians from the interior; shouting, bargaining, and deep in business—a perfect Babel.

The hotel-keeper, a young man, received me and my native helper very kindly. We went out to sell, and in a short time nearly all our Bibles, portions, etc., were disposed of. A crowd gathered, they had heard of us, and came to know about the truth. Question followed question in quick succession.

" Is confession to priests biblical ? "

" Should mass be heard ? "

' What is purgatory ? "

" How can a man be saved ? " and so forth.

We went to the hotel, where we sang Gospel hymns to these dear people, and read and explained the Scripture. It was 2 a.m. when we retired.

Through the kindness of our hotel keeper we obtained a house for Sunday services. Our first meeting was announced for 3 p.m., but by 12 the street was full of people anxiously awaiting the appointed time. Eagerly and most attentively did they listen to the story of JESUS, hearing for the first time in their lives how much He loved them, what He had done for them, and why He had come to this world. . . . Tears were seen coursing down many a cheek. All listened profoundly, with eager faces and bent heads. It seemed as if the SPIRIT of GOD was waking them from a long, long sleep.

After speaking for about three hours we said we had finished for that day because we were very tired; but many refused to leave until we promised to continue our meeting in the evening in the hotel. They returned in double numbers a little later—the evening meeting lasted till 1 a.m.

Monday was a saint's day, and the priest, being furious with us, had announced his intention of giving a sermon against Protestantism. Few went, but we learnt that after the priest had given his sermon, condemning Protestants generally, and Luther and Calvin in particular, a man in the audience got up and retaliated by coolly telling the priest that he was not speaking truth.

The President of the Municipal House, who had been very friendly to us, and had purchased a Bible and several tracts, was met by the priest, who expostulated hotly.

"How could you buy a Bible without the bishop's permission? How can you countenance Protestants, who are deceivers?" etc. "*Sur, padre, eu tambem tenho juizo e uma consciencia,*" calmly replied the president.—"Sir priest, I also have judgment and a conscience."

At 3 p.m. we had another and still larger meeting. After speaking on 1 Corinthians i. 17, 18, trying to set forth the excellency of the Gospel of JESUS CHRIST my friend the Colonel handed up a paper on which were written about a dozen questions, which he wanted us to answer. The following are some of them :—

How will sinners be punished?

Is there a way of escape from this punishment?

What can a man do to be saved?

How many Saviours are there?

What is the use of the confessional?

What is the use of mass?

This meeting lasted late into the night, and after we had finished, many followed us into the hotel, inquiring about the truth.

On Tuesday we had to return to Bahia. You can imagine how hard it was to leave these dear people. Gladly would we have stayed at Amargosa and preached the Gospel of life, but duty compelled us to return to our own work.

*When will Brazil have the Gospel?*

The people are longing for the truth ; groping in the dark.

Oh, if you could but have had a peep at our audience—at the dark, sincere faces wetted by tears of grief because of their sins ; if you could have seen, even for a moment, the sad little party who left us at the railway station, pleading with us to return, your heart would be touched, and gladly would you deny yourself to send the Gospel to Brazil.

As in starting we thanked the President of the Municipal House for his many kindnesses, he answered,—

" Nay, we have to thank you for bringing the truth to us ! "

Will you not, dear reader, help to send that truth to this neglected land ?

## Part II. The Land of the Holy Cross.

What has been done for the country from which this appeal comes? Has it a claim on us?

(RIO DE JANEIRO, THE CAPITAL OF BRAZIL.)

BRAZIL. What a vast unknown lies behind the word! Comprising one-fifteenth of the land surface of the globe—twenty-one States, the smallest of them larger than Belgium, and the rest varying from the sizes of Denmark, Greece, Portugal and Great Britain, up to those of Germany, Austria, Persia and Thibet—this "land of the Holy Cross"[1] has within the last five years been transformed from the noblest empire of the New World into the youngest-born American Republic.

[1] The name Brazil is derived from the Portuguese *Braza*, a live coal, a name taken from the colour of Brazilian dye-woods. The first name given to the country by its discoverers was *Terra da Santa Cruz*, "the land of the Holy Cross."

Discovered in the spring of A.D. 1500 by the Portuguese Pedro Cabral, it fell into Portuguese [1] and Romish hands, and was for 300 years cut off from all the world, almost as completely as China and Japan, by Portuguese policy. But just as in North America a century and a half of transatlantic life prepared the descendants of the Puritans for independent existence, three centuries of Portugo-Brazilian history produced a modified race [2] disposed to throw off the yoke of the old *régime*, and in 1822 a change that had long been pending came to pass— Brazil claimed independence. The action sprang from a royal source, the son of the king of Portugal becoming the first Emperor of Brazil.

CONTINENTAL PARTING-LINES BETWEEN THE SPANISH AND PORTUGAL DOMAIN
Scale 1 : 60,000,000

SPANISH AND PORTUGUESE S. AMERICA. [1]

---

[1] On its discovery S. America was divided between Portugal and Spain, Portugal taking Brazil, Spain all the rest, except the Guianas. In 1578 Brazil was conquered by Spain, and Dutch influence was subsequently paramount; but in 1654 Portugal again secured the country, and successfully maintained her rule till 1822, when the Braganza house was founded.

[2] Result of (1) change of climate, (2) introduction of the negro element, marriage among the Portuguese, natives and negroes, lessening the purely Latin section, and introducing the Mestizoes, who much retard social and political progress.

Nine years later the constitution forced upon him being too liberal, he abdicated in favour of his five-year-old son, Don Pedro II., who ruled under a regency till 1840, and terminated half a century's reign in November, 1889, by resigning his sovereignty "under constraint."[1] There was a bloodless revolution, and after more than sixty years' gradual emancipation the nation became self-governing.

With the Republic came disestablishment, liberty of religion, and the abolition of slavery.[2] Up to Sunday, May 12th, 1888, you hired your servants from an "owner," or bought and sold them as you did furniture. Now the two to three million negroes of Brazil are as free as those of the United States.

The natural wealth of the country is almost fabulous. Its river system is the finest in the world.[3] Its mountain chains[4] contain coal, gold, diamonds, silver, tin, zinc, mercury, and "whole mountains of the very best iron ore." Its Amazon forest covers a tract of level country 1,200 miles wide E. to W., 800 N. to S. The "stillness and sombre awfulness of these primeval woodlands can scarcely be conceived," and can only be compared to Mr. Stanley's discoveries "in Darkest Africa." Coffee, tobacco, rubber, sugar, maize, cocoa, rice, beans, cassava and quantities of cattle-sustaining grass from the inland *llanos*[5] and *selvas*,[6] are freely grown. The annual exports amount to £16,000,000, fruit and food being equally easily raised.

In 1873 the Brazilian Government had organised on their great natural water highways nearly 1,200 miles of interior steam navigation. Over six

---

[1] Since the recent death of Don Pedro and his queen, the Princess Isabella, daughter of Don Pedro II., and wife of Count D'eu, claims the right to the throne of Brazil for her son.

[2] The act of liberation was carried by the Brazilian Parliament, Don Pedro being at the time in Europe. In popular opinion the Princess, who signed the Liberation paper, freed the slaves.

[3] Leaving the Amazon out of account, the Xingu is 1,200 miles long, the Madeira 2,050.

[4] Three principal mountain ranges: The *Serra do Mar* or Sea-range, 5,000 feet high; the Serra Espinhaço, rising to 7,000 feet, and the Vertentes, whose highest peak is estimated at 10,000.

[5] Plains.          [6] Marshes.

thousand miles of railway have been opened up; and 17,400 miles of telegraph line connect various parts of the Republic: while a transatlantic cable links its populous towns and scattered ranches with the Old World. The climate is tropical, varying from the temperate south[1] and salubrious uplands to the malarious river courses and seaboard. All kinds of wild animals breed and range in the interior,[2] in parts even encroaching on the domain of man. "No country has more flowers, and none more precious stones; no country exceeds it in natural fertility, yet in few countries is agriculture more neglected." And few have been as much ruined and retarded by human sin and weakness as Brazil.

---

[1] In Southern Brazil it is frequently even cold, the thermometer falling to 40° Fahrenheit, and occasionally even to freezing point. São Paulo usually numbers 235 days of brilliant sunshine during the year. In some northern districts no rain falls at times for two and three years together. Intermittent fever is common during the terrible dearth resulting. The Brazilian rainy season is equivalent to the European winter.

[2] Brazil has been called the naturalist's paradise. Its innumerable varieties of butterflies, beetles and insects are only equalled by its multitudinous reptiles and its game—opossums, hares, partridges, ducks, deer, wild cats, pumas, etc. Thinly peopled by Indian tribes, its forest has but few creatures, but the boa constrictors in the rainy season are so numerous that specimens wandered from their forest home have sometimes been killed in the towns.

The 16,000,000 people of this newly-made Republic have had no Bible for 300 years, and their condition is a fair test of the results of Romanism *per se*—veneer and soulless externality in religion, a stiff jewel-encrusted ecclesiasticism, side by side with gross immorality. Such open license exists that a Brazilian judge recently sued in court a man who had bribed him and failed to pay the bribe.

Among the leaders of thought and policy a general decay of religious conviction is flinging wide the doors to spiritism,[1] positivism, modern free-thought, and sin, while the ignorant are bound by degrading superstition.

"Travelling through Paraná in S. Brazil, Mr. H. Maxwell Wright visited the small town of Tibagy, famous for its '*monje*,' or monk. There, in a shed at the back of a small farm, half sitting, half reclining on a mat and a skin of some wild animal, was a man of about seventy years of age in a state of nudity, a small piece of red blanket thrown over his shoulders barely covering them. His whole body was encrusted with filth, and his nails grown like claws; his vacant look showed him to be a poor helpless idiot. Beside him, a large wood fire was kept burning, the ashes of which, strewn round him for the sake of cleanliness, are carried away for medicinal purposes by the thousands of pilgrims, men and women, who come from long distances to see him, in the full persuasion that he is a holy man and has miraculous powers!"

What would our lives be—what would our national life be—if for ten years the Bible was blotted out?

What must be the condition of this nation that for 300 years has been without the Word of GOD? The Church of Rome allows her votaries no conscience, no independent thought. Generations bound by her mental and moral slavery have produced the Brazilian of to-day. Forbidden to have opinions, he has learned to do without; has become an indifferentist in spiritual things, and has given free rein to his lowest passions. So that this magnificent country, with a coast line 4,000 miles long, and a breadth of 2,500 miles,[2] dowered by nature with almost unparalleled wealth of animal

---

[1] Spiritism especially abounds. Every town has its *centros*, or club, with medium and *séances*.

[2] Length of Brazil, 2,600 miles N. to S.; 2,500 miles E. to W. Atlantic to the Andes. Area, over 3,000,000 square miles, 270,000 sq. miles more than the U.S.A., excluding Alaska.

THE FORBIDDEN BOOK.
From the Painting by M. Karel Ooms.
"A nation for 300 years without the word of God" (see previous page).

and vegetable life and mineral treasure, is peopled by a weak, immoral race, unable to develop its resources, or to cope with the difficulties of its government.

Spiritually, Brazil is a nation in the balance. Her people are passing through a period of transition. Slavery, state-churchism, and royalty have gone. Shall Romanism go too?

The general loosening of ideas that came with the Republic produced two effects, helping and hindering Christian work. Disestablishment opened the door to the hearts of the people. And liberty of faith has come.

"We can preach what we please, we can go where we like, we can publish what we please. We have freedom of press ; freedom of religion ; freedom of conscience," writes a missionary : " there is a loosening of old ties ; a wonderful stir among the people. Crowds gather wherever the Gospel is proclaimed."

But, on the other hand, Rome is upon her mettle, and she has much at stake. Disestablished, she is not yet disendowed ; though a gradual extinction of monastic and conventual establishments is in process by legal enactment.

" All that I saw of the Church of Rome in Brazil," writes the Rev. M. H. Houston, " her processions, her sacred places, impressed me with the vigour of the efforts she is making to tighten her hold on the people. Her separation from the State was hailed by us as a token of good : but there are two sides to the case. The Church, thrown on the voluntary contributions of the people for support, is doing her utmost to win their favour. Roused from indifference and weakness, she is compelled to organize, and at no period during the present half-century has Rome presented so bold a front in Brazil as now."

The present is a crisis of opportunity. " The old is broken up, what the new shall be it is ours under GOD to determine."

And what are we doing for Brazil ?

Among the sixteen millions of this vast young republic we are at the present moment maintaining one missionary.

" You ask," writes Mr. Fanstone,[1] " about the English Christian workers in Brazil. At present I know of but one who is working among the natives. There is in Rio, and also in Pernambuco, a man working among British seamen in the Ports. In Rio, Mr. Williams ; in Pernambuco, Mr. Holms. I know of no other than Mr. McCall who is paid by any English Society to work among Brazilian people."

Six American Societies, with about forty ordained missionaries, are in the field ; and Mr. H. Maxwell Wright, Mr. Fanstone, and a few others from this country have done evangelistic and pastoral work at their own charges ; but among the sixteen millions of Brazil we are at present maintaining only one missionary.

---

[1] See *Help for Brazil*, page 175, Appendix. In June, 1894, three months after Mr. Fanstone's letter was written, he returned to Pernambuco with four new workers.

Why are we not reaching these multitudes?

Have we ever given Brazil even a thought or prayer? Let us, in the presence of our SAVIOUR JESUS CHRIST, give it now, at any rate, a few minutes' earnest attention, seeking to realize what lies behind the following experiences of one who has spent years in evangelistic effort among the Portuguese-speaking people of the Peninsula, the Azores and Brazil.

### Part III. Do=able, but not Done.

#### NOTES FROM AN EVANGELIST'S EXPERIENCE.

"SO-AND-SO has taken the LORD," or, "The LORD has gone to So-and-so." Every one familiar with Brazil is familiar with this expression. It means that "So-and-so" is sick, and that the Romish wafer has been carried to the house. Here the people's only idea of CHRIST and GOD is that wafer which they constantly eat and profit nothing by. Rome puts Church, priest, mass, crucifix, Madonna — everything — between the soul and CHRIST.

"Is this worth buying?" said a young girl, taking a hymn-book from our colporteur package. "It's all Christ, Christ, Christ, Christ! I do not want it," she exclaimed, after glancing at its contents.

"*All Christ!*" How unknown the word and the reality are in Brazil!

I have travelled in this country, 1,000 miles up the Amazon, and on my last evangelistic trip covered 8,000 miles, preaching almost every night. My

I

recent tours have been especially along the four lines of railway which run in-land from Pernambuco, and give access to large numbers of towns. At none of these is any Gospel work being attempted. I have found it an excellent plan to give Gospels in the railway carriages, thus gathering groups of listeners who are glad to be read out loud to. Over 700 Gospels and thousands of tracts were sold in this way.

The present openings and facilities are truly wonderful. Since the proclamation of religious liberty, many of the officials are ready to grant halls anywhere, and, indeed, seem to feel that they can't refuse. In one small place, Perguica, some distance inland, when we arrived late in the day, the dancing saloon was at once granted us, free. Of course no announcement of the meeting had been made, but I happened to have with me a walking advertisement in the person of an old planter—an ex-desperado, who used to go about with a bowie knife, and had been prominent in all political rows. Since his conversion, his one idea is to spread the knowledge of CHRIST. His method of making the meeting known was singular, but effective.

" You must come and hear this man," he would say. " This is not an ordinary man ! The Government knows this man, gives him halls, theatres, preaching places as many as he likes."

It was useless for me to try to stop him.

A large crowd collected outside, looking through the doors and windows of the saloon, and by-and-by came in. We had good meetings. At the close of the second an old man came up to me, saying :—

" I want to have a long talk with you. If what you say is true, I am utterly wrong. I am trusting in what is of no avail. I have been brought up to believe that the consecrated wafer is the very body of CHRIST, and that in adoring it we adore GOD Himself. If what you say is true, my trust is false ! "

" Don't mind what I have said," I answered ; " go and see if what you believe is in the Word of GOD or not."

We had some conversation, and he promised to come next day, but was somehow prevented. I wondered why, as I was obliged to leave the town that day for Catende, where we had a good gathering. There was no hall available, so I spoke in the open air to a large and attentive crowd. Coming down the line next day to Palmares, I went into the town, and found, after coming away, that I had to return to the station for letters that had been overlooked. Feeling tired and unwell (a serious attack of fever came on that night), I wondered why I was thus obliged to go back, but understood when I met my old friend at the station. He was evidently delighted to see me, and exclaimed, "Can't we have some conversation?"

"Yes," I said; "come into the waiting-room."

We talked for over an hour. I took him through the whole New Testament on the great central theme of Atonement, from the last supper at Jerusalem to the "one sacrifice for sins for ever" of Hebrews x. He was wonderfully interested, and astonished at having lived so long without hearing these things.

Later on in the day I was speaking to a man at a street window. My new friend, who is a schoolmaster by calling, stood by listening to the Brazilian's rapid talk. The latter was quoting in an excited way what the Church taught about the value of the intercession of the Virgin and saints. When he paused, the old man said gravely,—

"Ah, but isn't the one question for you and me to settle—'What does GOD teach in His word?' If it is not what CHRIST taught, of what worth can it be?"

I never saw the old schoolmaster again. He was on his way to take up a new charge at an inland sugar plantation; and I, taken ill that night, and obliged to leave the country, could only send him a message with a Bible and some books. But I shall always have the unutterable joy of knowing that he had come to understand, as he said, "What CHRIST taught."

At Palmares the use of the Theatre or Literary Club had been promised, but when we arrived was refused. We tried to secure a large private room, but Catholic opposition prevented. Late in the day a man offered an empty corner-store, fronting the leading Church, and opening on to two streets. It was too late to announce the meeting, and when the time came we went down by ourselves. The place was dark and empty—a huge cavern-looking area, with a small table, a chair, and a lighted candle at one end. The church opposite, illuminated in honour of some saint, was filled with a congregation of women. For some time we had the store to ourselves.

"Stand in front," I said to my travelling companion, "and form a back for others to come and stand beside you."

He obediently ranged himself as my sole auditor, and very soon the people gathered, first a handful, then a score or two, till the place was full with some two hundred persons.

As the women left the church, they crowded round the doors (of which there were eight), and on the street, listening. I could not see the outskirts of the crowd ; indeed, little more than the front ranks of dark, southern faces, lit by the flickering candle-light, were visible. It was a winter night—such winter as you get in the tropics. Just before I began speaking, a messenger came, asking me to wait, as the Chief of Police was on his way down, and wished to be present. Nearly all the town officials, I afterwards learned, were there—lawyers, doctors, officers, and others, and to most, if not all of them, my message was probably new.

I waited for the chief, and then began, as we often have to in Brazil, going straight into the subject without prelude of hymn or prayer. I spoke for an hour, while they listened with wonderful interest, marks of approval here and there showing their grasp of the subject.

Could any mission sphere offer a wider open door ?

This experience at Palmares was in the north of Brazil, but the south and central districts offer similar opportunities. The Rev. G. W. Chamberlain, of Bahia, found the greatest encouragement in itinerating in the latter sphere.

In one place the priests bribed a number of rough fellows to waylay him (intoxicating them afterwards as a reward), but a group of the leading men of the place, hearing of their design, armed themselves and acted as a volunteer body-guard, escorting the American preacher from his hotel to the meeting. The priests, finding their attempt frustrated, went to the city magnates and urged them not to countenance the meetings ; but so far from acceding to this request, the latter begged Mr. Chamberlain to return and preach.

So much for the centre.

In the south, the Rev. H. C. Tucker found open doors everywhere. He travelled with two colporteurs,[1] and in connection with his American Bible Society work, rigged up a tent on the outskirts of the different towns, and found good sales and preaching opportunities.

At one place he sent his colporteurs alone into the city, and was presently astonished to see them returning more quickly than they went, a large crowd at their heels shouting, " Kill them ! kill them ! "

" My friends, listen to me," said Mr. Tucker, standing at the door of his tent and waving his hand to attract attention. And as soon as they were fully within hearing, he began to sing,—

" *O grande amor do meu Jesus,*"—" *The love that Jesus had to me !*" . . .

The change was extraordinary. The people listened spellbound to the hymn and address that followed. Forty Bibles were bought, and the quondam row ended in friendly feeling on both sides.

These three experiences, gathered from the north, south, and central States, show how ready the people are to listen everywhere in this vast and needy land.

Think of the scattered towns along the railway lines, on the open flats of the coast-land from Pernambuco north—and north of Pernambuco there is not a single Protestant worker—populated by from three to five or ten

---

[1] One, Antonio Marquez, is now training in the East London Institute, and hopes to return to evangelize in his own country.

thousand souls apiece.　They lie there, sandy stretches and palm trees, river and mangrove swamps, with big sugar-growing districts, filling the country between them.　Twenty or thirty miles inland the dense tropic forest begins and reaches everywhere, where not cleared ; but all along the roads you find houses every few minutes, with numbers of blacks, mulattos, and half-castes.

Go and speak to this countryman ; ask him,—

" Where is your soul going to ? "

SANDY STRETCHES AND PALM TREES, RIVER AND MANGROVE SWAMP.

" Where GOD likes," he answers, with an indifferent shrug.

" Where GOD likes ?　But GOD sent His Son to save the world, and CHRIST is waiting to save you ! " and as you tell him the good news, he listens for the first time with great astonishment.

I shall never forget the cry that went up from one poor soul when she first heard the truth.

" GOD forgive me, never again, never again ! " she exclaimed, trembling.

" To think that all these years I have been taking this wafer into me .
adoring it, thinking it was GOD! . . . . Never again ! never again !"

All her life she had hated Protestants, and would never listen to them.
She, however, came to a Gospel meeting, and the first time that she heard
her heart was " opened."

" But surely it is not a sin to pray to the Virgin, senhor ? " she said to me
one day. " I pray to the Virgin because I am such a poor sinner. Perhaps
CHRIST would not receive me, but *she* has a tender heart."

" If you were sick," I replied, " would you send for the doctor, or for the
doctor's mother ? "

" I see now !" she cried, as I explained my illustration.

Shall not these souls be reached ?

If men are wanted for the banks or the telegraph in Rio de Janeiro, or
to lay some railway into the interior, or to push the sale of the latest pro-
duction in the way of soap, there are plenty ready to go—and Christian men
too—in spite of the yellow fever ; and there is no lack of money—" *It's
business !*"

But to send to perishing sinners the glad tidings of salvation through
our LORD JESUS CHRIST, is not a " business " out of which people can make
money, and so few care to embark in the enterprise. " *We do nothing else
with so little zeal, self-sacrifice, and energy, as we do the Lord's work, and no
fact is more humiliating !*"

" Go out quickly into the streets and lanes of the city," said the lord
to his servant ; and the servant said, " Lord, it is done."

" Go ye into all the world, and preach the Gospel to every creature : "
into the heart of China and the centre of Africa ; up the Niger, the Congo,
the Amazon ; into *all* the world, to *every* creature, said our LORD, 1,800 years
ago. And can we say, " Lord, it is done " ?

Can we say we have done our best ?

Can we even say we have done something ?

SKETCH MAP OF SOUTH AMERICA,
WITH GREAT BRITAIN ON THE SAME SCALE

## CHAPTER VI.

### THE STATES OF THE WEST.

*"Henceforth that place is my home where I can have the greatest opportunity of labouring for my Saviour."—Tholuck.*

WHEN, three centuries ago, the Spaniards, sailing unknown seas in search of spoil and glory, landed on the western coasts of South America, Europe for the first time touched the Pacific seaboard of the New World, and found there, instead of savages, one of the most highly-organized civilizations history has seen—the Empire of the Incas, ruling from Chili to Colombia, over the Ecuador, Peru, and the Bolivia of to-day. Enriched by the accumulated wealth of centuries, and practising a social and industrial system which the shrewdest of our political economists could scarcely improve, the Incas boasted, besides their own remarkable palaces and temples, a series of wonderful architectural remains,[1] dating from a still more remote antiquity.

[1] The sun-circles of Scandinavia and Tartary, the stone-circles of Carnac in Brittany, and Stonehenge and Avebury in England, find their counterparts in the stone-circles of Peru. From these simple architectural efforts, common alike to Europe, Asia, and America, the constructive genius of the Peruvian tribes developed the colossal structures of Tiahuanaco, whose mysterious ruins stand to this day south of Titicaca. From the earth huts of the ancient Britons to St. Paul's, the distance in time and progressive effort is not, perhaps, greater than from the stone huts of the early Sierra dwellers to these fortresses and temples. The hard stones composing them have been cut, and their geometrical ornaments and carved figures designed and executed with wonderful technical skill.

"I may say once and for all, carefully weighing my words, that in no part of the world have I seen stones cut with such mathematical precision and admirable skill as in Peru."—Mr. E. G. Squier, *Incidents of Travel and Exploration in the Land of the Incas.*

"THE SPANISH CHRONICLERS."

Of the civilization that produced these triumphs no trace but their silent monuments is left to the world. And of the subsequent Inca dynasty not much remains beyond the traditions of the Spanish chroniclers, and the cyclopæan structures left by the Sun-children themselves— built of huge irregular blocks of stone, so admirably cut and jointed that to this day the point of a knife cannot be inserted between them. The Incas possessed no alphabet or written language ; and the secret of their *quippu* system—by which memoranda of national transactions were kept in knotted cords, the character of the events being indicated by the colour of the cords, the size and distance of the knots, etc.—has long since been lost. A forgotten era, chronicled only by mighty monuments of ruined stone, an echo among the soundless halls of the dead, the memory of their day survives strangely in this upstart century.

The Empire of the Incas fell before the Spanish crown, and became feudatory to the Pope. The headquarters of the Inquisition were set up at Lima, and the third era in the story of Western South America began. Little good came of the new-comers, whose main idea was rather to get than to give.

Their vices and their wars destroyed millions.  Their thirst for gold ruined the
Inca temples by plunder, fire, and sword.  Misery, dissatisfaction, and revolt
followed, but without redress, till the nineteenth century wave of revolution
swept across from Europe and transformed the New World as it had done
the Old.  In 1820 the western States, rising about the same time as Brazil,
abolished the Inquisition and threw off the foreign yoke, ending in the half-
dozen republics of to-day their four historic epochs.[1]

From that time their watchword has been PROGRESS.  The power of the
priests has been weakened in most of the large towns.  Half Spanish South
America has declared religion free, and even in Peru, Bolivia, and Ecuador,
there is hope of full emancipation.[2]

Through political convulsions, almost as frequent as their earthquakes,[3]
the western States are moving forward.  Their constitutions are modelled on
that of the United States ; and with presidents, senates, deputies, electors,
standing armies and navies, and large national debts, they are taking their
place among modern nations, and, judging from their natural advantages,
have an important part yet to play.

Few countries in the world can compare for wealth and beauty with the
western seaboard of South America.

"The spectacle presented to the stranger on landing in Peru is enchanting.  His gaze
is at once and above all irresistibly fascinated by the gigantic range of the Cordilleras,

---

[1]  1) Their early, prehistoric, but high civilization ; (2) the INCA dynasty, which, rising in the eleventh century, at-
tained its greatest extension and supremacy at the time of the discovery of America by Columbus, and fell before Pizarro,
in 1532 ; (3) the SPANISH rule and misrule, from the sixteenth to the nineteenth centuries ; (4) the present century's
REPUBLICS.

[2]  Early in 1894 a band of missionaries and teachers of the Methodist Church sailed from New York for Peru.  The
party included the Rev. Thomas B. Wood, presiding elder of the South American Conference, who carried a petition to
the people and Governments of Ecuador, Peru, Bolivia, and Chili to reform their constitutions in favour of religious
liberty.  Certificates of authority were signed by the Secretary of the State of New York, and by the Secretary of the
State Department of Washington, and he hopes that the four republics would grant the petition.
     The other six republics of South America—Chili, the Argentine, Uruguay, Paraguay, Venezuela, and Colombia—
have incorporated freedom of worship in their constitutions.

[3]  During its first twenty years of freedom, Peru made five and rejected four constitutions, those of 1822, '26, '27, 34,
and '39.  Its political turmoil was relieved by the abolition of slavery in 1854.

apparently rising sheer out of the water, their precipitous, rocky walls and jagged crests varied with deep, sharply defined mountain-gorges. . . . . . The outlines of these enormous ranges rise one behind the other in the blue, hazy distance, a wild confused chaos of crests, ridges, rugged crags, and clefts, between which, here and there, hover dark lowering masses of clouds, banked up against the mountain sides. And when one of these

COTOPAXI, THE SOUTH AMERICAN "IDEAL VOLCANO."
*Its large crater is still in constant commotion.*[1]

is occasionally rent asunder, there are disclosed to the view broad and glittering snow-fields, beyond which lie still other and far more distant jagged peaks, towering to the amazing heights, supreme giants amid the chaotic surroundings."

Gold, silver, copper, lead, and other ores are buried among these moun-

---

[1] In 1877 the torrent of mud and *débris* thrown off by Cotopaxi moved at a rate of over half a mile a minute, reaching the sea, 180 miles away, on the day of the eruption.

tains.[1]  At some of the highest elevations of the Andes, scarcely trodden by human footsteps, it is hardly possible to pass half a day without discovering rich streaks and veins of untouched mineral wealth.

The coast lands are rainless.  In some parts no rain has fallen within the memory of man.  Gloomy clouds overhead ; a line of white surf along the shore, edging the Pacific ; this arid seaboard, lifeless, save for the strip of verdure that hems its river banks and scattered seaports, lies like an oven, its intense heat dispelling the sea dews that float in the rarefied upper air, and are drifted by the west winds to the Andes.  The central upland regions are sterile, and dead—save for the condor that is lord above, and the *vicuna*, sole denizen below.  Between the Sahara-like *punas*[2] lie valleys as luxurious as any in Italy.  Stupendous heights like Cotopaxi stand out among the Andes, and beyond the mountains eastward towards Brazil, vast *montanas* plains stretch, dense with primeval forests, running 5,500 feet up the mountains' rifted sides.

"These eastern plains," writes Colonel Church, "are capable, when cleared and tilled, of becoming the garden of the world."

But to-day they are densely overgrown with vast and cumbrous forests, no unfit illustration of the heavy overgrowth of Romish superstition, ignorance, and blind ceremonial which shroud in spiritual gloom the eight or nine millions of these western States.

Behind them lies a long, sad reign of mediæval darkness.

Before them—what ?

The CHRIST-illumination of a Spiritual Empire to be ?  A spiritual " *garden of the world* " ?

 *       *       *       *       *

---

[1] The area of the mountain district of Peru alone has been roughly estimated at 200,000 square miles ; the medium height of its Andes at 17,000 feet ; and of its Cordilleras, a vast chain running parallel to the Andes, north and south, at 11,000 feet above the sea-level.  Terrific peaks, like that of Chiquibamba, 22,000 feet high, and of the volcano Omati, whose gigantic summit towers 18,000 feet above the sea, stand out in solitary grandeur amid eternal snows, sinking our European heights into insignificance.          [2] Bleak, lofty tablelands.

" No mission field that I ever saw or heard of seems to me so full of unique interest as this old Inca Empire," writes Dr. Thomas Wood, of the American Methodist Mission, who has spent twenty-two years in South America. " There are millions of aborigines, retaining the peculiarities that characterised them before the European conquest, modified by a steady degeneration ever since that time, until this region, from being the brightest in all the Western Hemisphere, morally and religiously has become the darkest, and the hardest to reform. But the time is apparently near for a great awakening, and when it comes, the movement will take in the three Republics of Peru, Bolivia, and Ecuador—the land of the Incas—with a grand sweep.

" At present Mr. Penzotti and myself, with our families, and the colporteurs and local preachers working under our direction, form the only evangelising agency in all this old empire.

" We have already in the Church in Callao members to whom the Quichua is vernacular, and who can be made useful in reaching the masses of the interior. We have a man now operating experimentally in the Department of Cajamarca, with encouraging results. We have lately had two women make an evangelistic tour through the department of Junin, one a native of that department, and the other of Cuzco, whose adventures would form a thrilling story. We have two men in Bolivia, making its chief city, La Paz, a centre of operations for that part of the field.

" Efforts in Ecuador have demonstrated the impossibility of permanent occupancy as yet, but the possibility of doing there what we are doing elsewhere, by patient and persistent use of the same means. All the railway lines, from Antofagasta northward, have been canvassed, embracing more than a thousand miles of the coast belt ; and preparations are being made to penetrate the parts of the interior that are not yet reached by the railways.

" Come over and help us ! " he concludes. " The great future of Gospel work in these lands embraces not only the evangelisation of the native masses, but also the religious development of the new population destined to inundate them by-and-by, and fill them with mining and agricultural colonies of foreigners. Now is the time to work on the masses, before the new tide sets in. It will be doubly difficult to effect their moral regeneration after that tide is once in flow; be doubly difficult to deal with that tide if its incoming finds the native masses in their present immoral condition. The KING's business here requires haste.

"The perplexities of the work are bewildering to a degree that I never encountered before; yet, all in all, the encouragements seem to justify looking for success as sure, and expecting that when it comes in its fulness it will be grand. The possibilities of this field, as well as its difficulties, seem as colossal as the Andes."

What of the men and women of these western States?

Glance for a moment at Lima, the capital of Peru. A square-built city, flat-roofed, planned on the

A PERUVIAN LADY.

American right-angle system, it looks from the near heights much like a chessboard for regularity—a grey chessboard amid grey surroundings. Its principal buildings are superior in style, and its cathedral exceptionally fine, but much of the old town is built of sun-dried mud, which lasts in this rainless land.

"It is altogether a picture painted *en grisaille*—grey blocks of houses, grey churches and cloisters, grey hills, whose cloud-capped summits alone are clothed with a scarcely perceptible light green mantle of grass. The sky itself seems to partake of this monotonous grey tone, being overcast almost from one end of the year to the other.

"Nowhere is there to be seen a more motley population than that met with in its streets. The main elements are the whites, Indians, blacks, and Chinese, but the different shades of the various cross-breeds between these races can neither be enumerated nor described, so thoroughly intermingled have they become one with another. The contingent supplied by the *Cholos*, half-caste Indians and blacks, has undergone profound variation, and it is this class that mainly swarms in the squalid slums of the suburbs.

"A number of vessels convey every year crowds of coolies from China to Callao.[1] These wretched creatures bind themselves by contract for eight years, at a very low rate of remuneration, to the *Uencadados*, or planters, after which they again become their own masters. They are treated more or less as slaves, which, strictly speaking, they really are, there being no legal impediment of any sort to their sale, or rather, to their being consigned to any third party."

Try to realize the existence of these people.

We have not seen them—but what difference does that make? Six weeks' journey away from us, 6,000 miles distance across the Atlantic and Brazil, they are just as real as if they lived in Liverpool or Leicester. Is there no shame to us in the fact that *if they lived in Liverpool or Leicester we should carry them at once the message of God's love and free salvation, but simply because they live in Lima we forget them?*

They are living and dying there in darkness, "having no hope, and without GOD in the world." Say they were all here in our own Yorkshire— the population of Peru alone would fill the county, outnumbering the people now in it. Fancy them, in the heart of our sunny England. Halifax

---

[1] The port of Lima.

and Wakefield, with their busy manufactories and handsome homes, are exchanged for the mud walls of LIMA. PUIRA, with its 7,000 souls, is exchanged for Ripon; HUACAVELICA, with its 5,000, stands in place of Knaresborough. For our seaport Bridlington substitute TRUXILLO, with its

13,000 souls ; for Richmond and Settle, LAMBAYEQUE, and its 8,000 ; for Skipton, AYACUCHU'S 26,000. AREQUIPA, six times destroyed by earthquake and as often rebuilt, and containing to-day over 20,000 souls, may stand for Scarborough; while Pontefract and Northallerton are outbalanced by the 40,000 of CUZCO. We have plenty of people left for the townships and villages.

And now, having peopled the county, plunge them all in dense moral darkness.

ROMAN CATHOLICISM ?

Yes. But Roman Catho-

THE UNREACHED STATES OF THE WEST. licism *at home*.

Not as here, in the search-light of Protestant civilization, modified and Anglicised, but in all its native mediæval corruption and ignorance. "The Church is immensely rich. The archbishop at Lima is at the head of four suffragans, the bishops of Arequipa, Truxillo, Cuzco, and Ayacuchu. Curates and clergy abound, but their *morale* is not creditable to the profession. Morality is not high. The habits of the upper classes are luxurious, frivolous and idle ; the national temperament is passionate, and the metropolis is one of the gayest and grossest capitals in the world.

"The native Indians, about 350,000 in number, are uncared for by the Government in every sense—religious, educational, and political. The ' priests ' of the provincial districts are habitually drunken, extortionate, and ignorant."

Amongst the motley population of this new Yorkshire, here in our sunny England, are tribes of uncivilized Indians worshipping the moon, and dreading a demon called Nugi, whom they regard as the source of calamities. They have no chief, except when at war with their neighbours, when he who possesses most courage or cunning is elected. The Cara-panchas and Chipeos, two of these tribes, are almost European in physique, fair-skinned and ample-bearded, the women equal in beauty to Circassians. The Guaguas and Casibos are cannibals, and eat salt human flesh. The Iquitos are dexterous lancers, and adore rude images of quadrupeds, birds, and reptiles. The Yures are noted for their skill in poisoning. All these people, wandering on our Yorkshire levels and uplands—so put it for the moment—are "timid and dastardly from long oppression, melancholy by temperament, cowardly in danger, savage and cruel after victory, and severe and inexorable in the exercise of authority. They are great observers of the external rites and ceremonies of the Romish Church, and spend large sums of money in masses and processions—a species of profusion in which they are naturally encouraged by the priests."

Besides these pagans, the country is occupied by gambling and licentious Creoles, by Asiatic and European foreigners, Chinese coolies, and by Cholos, half-Indian, half-negro, an idle, ruffianly crew.

\*       \*       \*       \*       \*

They are not in Yorkshire, but they are within reach. And among them all, to-day—living, suffering, and dying in this same world of ours— there are only one or two ordained Protestant preachers of the Cross, with a group of young evangelists and teachers, not more than six or seven, all told.

K

If they were here as our next-door neighbours, should we not go to them? Could we refrain?

What difference does it make that they are across the sea?

*        *        *        *        *

We have compared Peru and Yorkshire. But Peru is only one of the western States. Eight times as large as England and Wales, its single western coast line over 1,000 miles long, and its eastern rich *montanas* stretching another 1,000 miles between the Andes and Brazil, it is more occupied and better known than inland Bolivia or exclusive Ecuador. But these, too, have their vast extent and their million-numbered nations. And neither of them has as yet a single missionary.

## ECUADOR AND BOLIVIA.

"ECUADOR," writes Mr. Charles H. Bright, of Lima, "is completely in the power of the Pope. He who is just now affecting a liberal policy in Europe, in Ecuador still rules with the iron hand of the middle ages. The Bible is declared contraband, and not allowed to pass the Custom House. No book or paper can be published that the 'Church' forbids. But there are people of liberal sentiments in some parts.

"No mission has ever attempted work in Ecuador.

"Its utter spiritual destitution seems all the more sad when we notice that it is, probably, the loveliest country of all South America."

The American Bible Society has attempted to reach the 2,300,000 of Bolivia, and had in 1893 three native colporteurs at work. Romish opposition is strong.

"Last year," writes Mr. Milne, the veteran superintendent of the Society's work in South America, "one of our colporteurs in Ayacuchu, had to make his escape by the roof of a house where he was staying, from a mob of half-castes, led on by a Friar. Finding their prey had escaped, they took his clothes and several boxes of Bibles to the plaza of the city, and burnt them."

Signor Penzotti's Bibles for colportage are, we hear by the last mail, at present confiscated by the Government, which in Bolivia, Peru and Ecuador still forbids the public exercise of any religion but Roman Catholicism.

COLOMBIA and VENE-ZUELA are more ad-vanced in civil and reli-gious lib-erty, but scarcely anything is being done for their 6,000,000 souls.

AMONG THE WESTERN MOUNTAINS.

"If," wrote Mr. Bright, after visiting Venezuela, "when the liberal reformer, Guzman Blanco, threw open the doors to Protestant missionaries, inviting them to enter Venezuela, and actually building a temple for Protestant worship (which was never occupied), they had only accepted the opening with zeal, oh, what might have been done! No response was made to Guzman's offer. When, at last, through the labours of unrecognised individuals, a little work was commenced in the capital, Guzman's influence was declining. The little work there continues, but *out-side the capital nothing has ever been attempted.*"

For the work of the Gospel, Venezuela may be divided into three regions.

1. "CARACAS, the capital, altitude 3,000 feet, with a beautiful spring-like, though enervating climate, and the neighbouring towns and coast easily reached. The coast towns are very hot and rather unhealthy, yellow fever being common, but they present the attraction of liberality of sentiment. Maracaibo is an exception to this rule. Here the fanaticism is extreme, and, besides, it is a deadly climate for foreigners.

2. "The important town of MÉRIDA, altitude 4,500 feet, with the adjacent healthy high lands. This is *untouched ground*, but there are printing presses and much intelligence, so that a prudent worker could easily establish a witness for CHRIST. From Mérida the thickly-populated districts of Colombia, a fine country, inhabited by a hospitable people, can be reached without descent to the coast.

3. "CIUDAD BOLIVIA, on the Orinoco, with the scattered tribes of Indians up the river, which might gradually be reached. The region is said to be healthy, though there is much chill and fever.

"The people of Venezuela are a mixture of Spanish and negro, with a very little of the Indian race. The Indians here do not mix with the European race, but have fled from the white man, and live retired and scattered."

"COLOMBIA," continues Mr. Bright, " is a very interesting field. With the exception of the coast, where the towns are few, it enjoys a healthy climate. The interior is, compared with other parts of South America, thickly populated. The Presbyterians have long been in Bogotá, the capital (8,000 feet high), but outside of this little has yet been done. The flourishing and thickly populated mountain valleys of the west are yet untried."

The Rev. M. E. Caldwell, of the American Presbyterian Mission referred to, has been working in the capital since 1880, and sends an earnest plea for help.

" In Bogota," he writes, " we have a little church of about 100 members, and two schools. For years we have been greatly hindered by lack of funds and labourers   .   .   .   .

" Romanism in its grossest form is the religion of the people. A very large part of the people can neither read nor write, and very few know anything about the Bible. The state of morals is sad beyond description. The majority of the intelligent and educated men have drifted away from Romanism, and are practically infidels. Many of these may, for political and social reasons, appear to be very good Catholics, and at the same time despise much that goes to make up Romanism.

" The ignorant and weak are under the power of a corrupt priesthood, and the intelligent and educated are, as a rule, completely under the influence of infidelity. They are a sad people, practically without GOD and without hope   .   .   ."

# CHAPTER VII.

## "AS SHEEP WITHOUT A SHEPHERD."—SOUTH AMERICA'S ABORIGINES.

"In the great eternity beyond, among the many marvels that will burst upon the soul, this surely will be among the greatest, that the Son of God came to redeem the world, that certain individuals were chosen out from mankind as a first-fruits, that to them was committed the inconceivable honour of proclaiming the glad tidings of salvation to their fellow-creatures still in darkness, and that they did not do it."—EUGENE STOCK.

S. AMERICAN INDIAN ENCAMPMENT.

WITH bone harpoons and flint-headed arrows the Fuegians creep along the indented shores of the southernmost islands of Cape Horn, seeking their daily food —miserable, naked, shivering creatures " who fifty years ago seemed almost to realize Charles Darwin's missing link before his eyes. Four thousand miles due north of dark Fuegia, Indian tribes roam amid the endless forests of the Amazon, tropical children of the same great family. Between the two lies the South American continent, appropriated by civilised European races who have ousted the children of the soil. And between these two extremities of their down-trodden race, five million pagan Indians, the last remnants of South America's aborigines, wander across the deserts of Patagonia, the prairies of Paraguay, and the Andes uplands, to which they have been driven from their ancestral lands.

No missionary view of South America can omit her oldest race. Among the most neglected of all her neglected children, her aborigines are dear to GOD. And surely we who sing, "I am Thine own, O CHRIST!" must feel some interest in these 5,000,000 souls "for whom CHRIST died,"

EARNEST COVE, SPANIARD HARBOUR, TIERRA DEL FUEGO.
*Scene of Captain Allen Gardiner's death, September, 1851.   See next page.*

some concern in the questions which this chapter is written to meet—

    I. *What has been done to bring them to* GOD?
    II. *What still remains undone?*

### I. WHAT HAS BEEN DONE FOR THE INDIANS OF SOUTH AMERICA?

Near Allen Gardiner's grave, round which the Cape Horn hurricanes raise requiem to the Fuegian Mission martyrs of forty years ago, Bishop

Stirling, of the South American Missionary Society, landed in 1869, and for seven months lived alone among the savage natives, daily expecting death. Three years later he baptized thirty Fuegians, and wrote of their meetings :—

"More touching, encouraging assemblies for prayer I never was at. The prayers were beautifully uttered, deeply reverent in tone, eloquent in expression, full of pathos."

The language of Fuegia, "a succession

FUEGIANS AND BARK CANOE NEAR CAPE HORN.

of guttural groans and grunts," now embalms the living word of GOD ; and these lowest aborigines of South America have passed into the fold of CHRIST.

Twenty years later, in 1888, the tribes of the Gran Chaco—a Paraguayan plain of 180,000 square miles—were reached by the same mission. Henricksen, the leader of the first band of workers, died in the field, but Mr. Barbrooke Grubb succeeded him, and is labouring to-day, with a few helpers, at a lonely mission here, among "many different nations," speaking different languages, some warlike and nomadic, others peaceful agriculturists, all unevangelised.

"A woman died the other day," he writes ; "the Indians requested me to bury her, and speak to the great SPIRIT. This was the first funeral I had been present at ; formerly they would not even show us a grave. The incantations usual on these occasions were given up at my request—a great victory, which I little expected. . . .

"Indian law required the death of the child of the deceased woman, a baby three months old. It was to be thrown alive into its mother's grave. . . . I pleaded with the people, inwardly appealing to the Friend of little children. I told them how angry the

A VILLAGE IN THE PARAGUAYAN CHACO.

great GOD would be. . . . At last they yielded, and I carried away the prize. . . "The opening in the Gran Chaco is the key to 2,000,000 perishing heathen."

Among these 2,000,000 there are only five witnesses for CHRIST.[1]

The Indians are friendly, confiding, and obedient.

"But what I regard as more remarkable still," writes Mr. Pride, "is the little effect,

---

[1] Mr. Barbrooke Grubb, the leader of the Mission, is assisted by Messrs. Hay and Pride, from the East London Institute, Mrs. Hay and Mr. Ball.

comparatively speaking, that the adjoining civilization, with its vice, has made upon them, though they have been so long near it. Even the coast tribes, which have come in contact with it most, and have suffered most from it, *have a moral code higher than that of the so-called civilized community.* At the present moment a young Indian belonging to Fernandez *toldo* is in banishment because he married again, his first wife being separated from him. Across the river such an occurrence would be winked at.

"It seems to me as if GOD's protecting hand has been over this people, and that He has been reserving them for Himself. They are without any religion or form of worship, but full of superstition, the stillness of the night often being broken by their endeavours to charm away devils or sickness by loud, weird, monotonous singing.

"Three nights ago, upon going into the boys' house, I found it full of men armed with guns and bows and arrows, while outside were scouts. They were watching for a spirit, described as very tall and very stout, which they supposed was without. *Unfettered by false religion, simple, generous, and confiding, they seem waiting for the knowledge of God.*"

Across the Andes, in Chili, a similar effort is contemplated by the same Society, as soon as funds and men are available. The tribes here are Araucanians, a finely developed, warlike race, to whom Allen Gardiner vainly sought access in 1838. Through the advance of civilization they have now become "everywhere accessible, and when not degraded by drink, form an important part of the population."

"In no part of South America," writes Bishop Stirling, "have I seen the Indians so numerous or so easy of approach. Their villages are in close proximity, they frequent in large numbers the fast-increasing frontier towns, and lie open to our touch in all directions. There is a manifest opening among them, an important opportunity, to miss which would be a grave mistake."

In 1889 the first missionary to Araucania, the Rev. J. R. Tyerman, a Spanish-speaking clergyman of the Church of England, provided with an iron church and mission house, went out. Sent primarily to the English colonists, he found the sphere encouraging, and gladly did what he could for the Indians around. Helpers were much needed.

"How thankful shall we be," he wrote, "when Mr. Gardiner arrives! He will be such a help to these poor people. Whilst I am writing, news comes of his arrival on the coast, so we hope to have him here soon.

The reference was to Mr. William Reade Gardiner, grandson of Captain Gardiner, who had gone out as a medical missionary almost at his own charges, to carry on the work in which his father's and grandfather's lives had been laid down.

GOD's ways are not as ours. March, 1891, brought the young missionary doctor to Valparaiso, and laid him in his grave. The same number of the Society's magazine which contained Mr. Tyerman's letter of welcome printed the notice of death.

"If only you could send me a helper like the late young Mr. Gardiner," wrote the isolated worker, "much more might be attempted; but as it is, I am a lone missionary in an out-of-the-way corner of the world. . . .

"If the Rev. Mr. Grubb from Keswick should penetrate thus far, he will have a hearty welcome."

But the recent Keswick mission fell short of Araucania, and the single-handed soldier still holds his post

THE LATE WILLIAM READE GARDINER.
*Grandson of Captain Allen Gardiner.*

alone. An unreached nation round him, he looks across the ocean to our crowded Christian lands.

"Oh that a rivulet at least," he writes, "of the great current of missionary zeal displayed in England, might find its way to the untouched fields of Araucania! *How long shall I be left here alone?*"

Beyond the three efforts we have mentioned, nothing is being done for South America's 5,000,000 aborigines. One worker and his wife occasionally reach some of the Chili natives; five are at work among the nations of Paraguay, and a group of thirteen among the vanishing races of desolate Fuegia. This is the list complete. Three little points of light influencing at the outside 50,000 heathen; 4,950,000 still unreached. And this after eighteen centuries of Gospel illumination and CHRIST-given command " to every creature."

## II. WHAT STILL REMAINS UNDONE?

Roughly speaking, the Indians of South America may be divided into five sections,[1] represented on the accompanying map by figures indicating the location of the leading races, and by varying density of shade, according to varying density of population. But for practical purposes we may divide the unevangelised aborigines of South America—excluding the Southern races, amongst whom some little work has been done—into two groups: the 3,000,000 Quichua-

MAP OF SOUTH AMERICA.
Showing approximately the location of the leading tribes of aborigines and their comparative numbers.

[1] I. ORINOCO RACES . . . . 1,450,000
(Caribs, Barré, Muiscas, etc.)
II. AMAZON VALLEY RACES . . 1,000,000
(Zupi, Jivaro, Zapáro, etc.)
III. PERUVIAN AND BOLIVIAN RACES . 1,500,000
(Quichuas, Moxos, Chiquitos, etc.)
IV. BRAZILIAN, SOUTH OF AMAZON . 1,000,000
(Guaranis, Guandos, etc.)
V. SOUTHERN RACES . . . . 250,000
(Araucanians, Puelches, Fuegians, etc.) ————
Total 5,000,000

For this approximate classification and estimate see BATES' *South America*. Stanford, London, pp. 555, 494, etc. See also BOLLAERT, and KEANE. The Quichua-speaking tribes of the West alone have recently been estimated at 3,000,000.

speaking Indians of the West (in Chili, Bolivia, Peru, and Ecuador), and the Amazon and Orinoco tribes.

## 1. THE 3,000,000[1] QUICHUA-SPEAKING INDIANS.

When, in 1527, the Spaniards landed in the west, they found the Inca empire ruling a simple aboriginal people, who welcomed the invaders with hospitality. In return the Spaniards "killed them, robbed them, and enslaved them without necessity and without motive, treating innocent creatures with the cruelty of hungry wolves, oppressing and destroying them by all the means they could invent. . . .  Greed of gold lay behind the horrid butchery. The conquerors knew no other god, and to fill themselves with riches they treated as vile refuse the people who received them as messengers from heaven."

"The ills," continues the historian Laz Cazas,[2] "that were suffered by the Indians were so many and so great that it is impossible to conceive of them."

"Unquestionably millions of the natives perished through wanton cruelties, and especially by the forced labour. . . .  They were literally worked to death. Their employment under the lash of the overseer in the mines and on the burning soil of the plantations, no doubt, also, the crushing burdens and weary marches of these 'pack animals' along rough mountain tracks, resulted in the rapid disappearance of nearly all those whom the conquest had delivered into the hands of white employers. Doubtless many tribes were able to avoid oppression by taking refuge in the mountains or the forests ; but they were unable to escape the fearful mortality caused by the epidemics following in the wake of the invaders. Thus, in the seventeenth century a great part of the natives perished."[3]

[1] "Fifty years ago, D'Orbigny computed the descendants of these Indian subjects of the Incas at barely half three millions ; but when we remember that the united population of Bolivia and Peru, to say nothing of Ecuador, is now computed at five and a quarter millions, of whom fifty-seven per cent. are pure Indians, and twenty-two per cent. Mestizos—mixed, also speaking Quichua, and that this is allowing Bolivia the same proportion of whites that the published statistics give to Peru, it will be seen that this estimate is much less than the reality."—A. M. MILNE.

[2] B. Laz Cazas, quoted in *La Historia del Peru bajo la Dinastia Austriaca*, by Sebastian Lorente, p. 2.

[3] Réclus, *South America, Universal Geography*, Vol. XVIII., S. Virtue, London.

At the time of this great mortality it was supposed that the western aborigines were destined to disappear. But history proved the contrary. After the period of decline the natives increased, some of the tribes advancing even at a more rapid rate than the whites, and to-day they display more vitality, more power of resisting the destructive forces, than the "red-skins" of North America. While the latter have either disappeared, or been for the most part swept into "reserves," the former still constitute the substratum of the population in the land of their forefathers.

They are as much as ever an oppressed, down-trodden race.

"Since the Spanish conquest," writes Mr. Milne, of the American Bible Society, "the progress of the Indian has been in the line of deterioration and moral degradation. Nor could it be otherwise : they are down-trodden by the landowners, who hold them as serfs ; they are wronged by corrupt authorities, who always give the right to the man who has money ; and they are oppressed by the Romish clergy, who can never drain contributions enough out of them, and who make the children render service to pay for masses for deceased parents and relatives.

"Tears came to our eyes as Mr. Penzotti and I watched them practising their heathen rites in the streets of La Paz, the chief city of Bolivia, some ten years ago. They differ from the other Indians in that they are domesticated, but they know no more of the Gospel than they did under the rule of the Incas.

"Yet all through Bolivia and Peru we find these half-castes eager to hear the Gospel and disposed to purchase the Scriptures, until their minds have been poisoned by the priests and friars."

As to their language, he continues :—

"The vast majority of the Indians cannot speak Spanish ; but the Cholos half-castes speak both Spanish and Quichua. The latter language prevails from Chili to Ecuador, a distance of more than three thousand miles. It has dominated the Spanish, and become the vernacular of the mixed race as it is of the Indians. In many parts it is generally spoken by the whites."

Civilization and Romish influence have begun to reach these simple people, but are proving a very doubtful good.

A recent traveller writes of the tribes in Ecuador :—

"Some people have formed such a flattering idea of the work of the Romish missions among the Indians, that they cannot conceive that as yet *nothing* has been done really intelligently adapted to the needs of this poor people.

"In former times the tribes were ingenious in work. The whites have imported the manufactures of Europe, and since then the women do not need to spin or weave, nor the men to make tools. They need only go to the river and wash out some gold to pay for cloth, knives, and trinkets. They have lost the custom of making any intellectual effort, and the whites not only have neglected to open their intelligences to more concrete ideas, but have drowned them in liquor.

"The white trader is generally a fugitive from society ; the Indian at once becomes his victim, and after being 'extortionised' and robbed for a long time, he himself at last becomes a bad man.

"Besides, the system of civilization put in practice with this poor people lacks all logic. For example, they wish to force the Indians to live, not in the forest, but in villages ; which certainly is a principle of civilized society. . . To accustom these men to live in one place they must be taught some useful trade ; but no such plan is followed. A church is built, the Indians are compelled to erect huts round it, and commanded to reside in the village thus formed.

"In such conditions how are they to subsist ?

"While enjoying liberty, they lived by the chase, and, somewhat, by agriculture ; they had their little forest patch of bananas and yuca ; with their poisoned arrows they killed birds and monkeys. But as soon as they are formed into a Romish 'mission,' they entirely lack the products of hunting. These villages are uninhabited most of the time ; the Indians return to the forest, and the houses that surround the church remain abandoned. From this continual troubles result.

"In 1875 the houses of the Panos Indians were burnt to force them to come and live in Archidona. But this brutal act, far from reducing them to obedience, made them obstinate rebels. They retired to the forests, where the whites never will be able to reach them.

"I have calculated that the cotton cloth sold to Indians in exchange for gold dust costs them fifty-three times dearer than in the retail stores in Guayaquil—that is to say, *two hundred and twelve times dearer than in France;* and yet the traders hardly ever get rich, because nearly all are drinkers and gamblers . . . a dissipated class, of no use to any one. For every reason I prefer the savage to them."

Romish priests are scattered here and there among these aborigines, but to what does their influence amount?

"To some of the settlements a *padre* comes once a year, and for several days religious ceremonies, attended with a considerable amount of dancing, eating, and drinking, are kept up. An altar is put up, and an image of the Virgin, with a light burning before it, from Saturday evening till Monday, so that, though there is no public service, the faithful can pass any portion of Sunday in adoration."

"The Spanish priests," writes Mr. Milne, "make no objection to the Indians practising their heathen rites, so long as they pay for masses and other ecclesiastical lies.

"The Gospel is the one and only lever that can raise them out of their misery. That it can accomplish this, there is no question. What the Gospel has done for others it can do for them. The only question is, Who will take it to them? For the Fuegian tribes—not numbering as many thousands as these do millions, and speaking languages that will in a few years be extinct —much has been done ; but, so far as we are able to learn, *the evangelization of the Quichua-speaking Indians has not been contemplated by any Society.* Will no missionary organization, will no follower of CHRIST, give some attention to the three million descendants of the subjects of the Incas, who speak one language, and one that can never die?"

## 2. THE INDIANS OF THE AMAZON.

Amid the impenetrable forests of the Upper Amazon, whose overhanging branches, intertwined with climbing plants, make it in some parts "impossible with an axe to clear a passage of more than a few paces," live another million Indians, unclad, untaught, unchristianised. On the banks of the Purus, a single tributary of the Amazon, there are thirty-two tribes whose names are known, and rumours of many more. Nothing could be more simple than the lives of these forest children amid the intense stillness of their primeval woods.

"Young and old leave their hammocks at sunrise, and pour water over their bodies with *cuias*, at the brink of the nearest stream. To procure and prepare food, and be constantly on the alert against mosquitos, venomous reptiles, scorpions, centipedes, poisonous ants, and, so forth, make up the duties of an ordinary day, and at sunset the hammocks are once more tenanted, and the village is hushed in slumber."

When young they are a handsome people ; the mothers, though deeply attached to their children, will bury alive a deformed or sickly infant.

INDIANS OF THE AMAZON FORESTS.

Threading the forest paths you come on an Indian village—small houses like beehives, the walls of tough stick, with palm-leaf roofs, and hammocks slung to poles their only furniture. Some large huts, shared by several families, measure seventy feet by twenty. On fibre mats spread on the muddy floor women and girls are sitting, with a look of settled gloom.

> " Ever and anon one of them slaps a mosquito on her leg or arm, or on her neighbour's back. All look far more haggard and weary than when they come freshly painted to the town. Home life is evidently a very melancholy affair . . . though there is no lack of food . . . plantains, fish, and flour in plenty, and a good stock of bows and arrows, harpoons and spears. Outside are pots and pans, and numerous shells of the turtles, which provide the staple article of diet."

Their tranquil lives run on to a great age. "One couple, as being too old to live," writes the missionary Clough,[1] "were turned out by their family at seventy, but they set to work, cleared a bit of land, built a canoe and hut, cultivated corn, cane, and tobacco, and jogged on comfortably together for another twenty years.

"They *loved each other*, there could be no mistake about it, and they were inseparable, the husband never stirring from the door without his wife, or the wife without her husband."

The man told Mr. Clough he trusted in the Mother of our LORD for salvation ; he knew nothing of CHRIST, except that He was the son of Maria Santissima.

They are a strong, courageous race, and like other nations demand that their youths should pass an ordeal before claiming the rights of manhood.

> " When the day arrives, amid the crash of drums, the young man steps boldly into a circle, and thrusts his arm beyond his elbow into a gourd filled with hornets, wasps, and tucandera ants (one sting of the last-named insect being enough to make a strong man almost faint). How eagerly his face is scanned by the assembly ! No cry of pain escapes between his clenched teeth, and blood might spurt from his pores before the gallant youth would show the white feather. The spectators do not delight in inflicting agony, but rejoice in seeing it bravely endured. . . . When the arm is withdrawn at the medicine man's signal, a huge bowl of intoxicating liquor is handed to him to drink, and partly to pour upon the ground as a libation, after which he is welcomed. Sometimes he falls and swoons with excruciating pain ; the women then nurse him, bring him round, and his mother unites her

---

[1] See *The Amazons*, by Mr. R. S. Clough, published by the S. American Missionary Society : 1, Clifford's Inn, Fleet Street, London.

voice with theirs in chanting over his senseless form : ' His heart is brave ! He knows not fear !' and so forth."

" Tell me about your home," asked Mr. Clough of a small Cashebo boy, who had been baptised at a Romish mission and taught Spanish.

" We lived in the forest," replied the child ; " we wore no clothes. I never saw clothes till I was captured. My father and uncle used to hunt and fish, my mother and aunts grew corn and manioc. I never was badly treated. We never killed anybody, but my father would kill Canibo men, women, and children, if he had a chance. He used to show us how to shoot men with the arrow. He used to shoot at a target, and call it a Canibo."

" Did you ever think about the spirit world ? "

" We believed in a good and a bad spirit. We thought we should go to a beautiful country after death, where there would be no enemies, and we should be able to catch turtles whenever we wanted them, and shoot monkeys without trouble. Sometimes my mother would cry, and say she wanted to go to the spirit world and be at rest. She lived in fear of enemies. We always were listening. One day we saw a canoe enter our lake, but as it went away we thought no one had seen us. Mother, however, was very anxious, and every now and then would jump and start.

" Three nights afterwards, when we were all asleep, people came suddenly into our house, and my father, mother, uncles and aunts were all run through with spears."

" You were very frightened ? "

" Yes, I was very sorry, and wanted to be killed, but my cousins and I were taken slaves by the Canibos, and from them I was bought for some goods. I am happy now. Sometimes I see in my dreams all that happened on that dreadful night."

" Do you want to go back again ? "

" No, I do not want to go back again ; I am happy here. I can croak like a frog ! "

".And then," adds Mr. Clough, "a variety of croaks were emitted. He was a wonderful child for his age; he could say the first two lines of the LORD's prayer, count twenty, and stand on his head alone."

To these forest aborigines the S. American Missionary Society sent workers in 1872, first on an exploring visit, and later on to settle on the Purus.[1]

"The care of native children and the necessary work of house-building, land-clearing, and so forth, at first occupied all the pioneers' time. In the course of 1880, however, they set out for a missionary journey to some of the higher tributaries of the Purus river. . . . They saw and talked with many Indians. . . . Mr. Clough found his friends still living from hand to mouth, as poor and uncultivated as ever, and with the same aspect of calm sadness.

"The Pamarys of Lake Ajarahan were revisited—people who live on rafts and *jangadas*—collections of tree trunks lashed together, sometimes moored, sometimes used for conveyance from place to place. A permanent hut on shore is never built by the Pamarys, and they say it has been so with them from time immemorial. They have a tradition that there was once a direful and universal deluge, that their ancestors escaped drowning by means of *jangadas*, and therefore the Pamarys always live now in readiness for any such great flood in the future."[2]

"Upon the tree trunks, floored with rough laths made from a certain straight-grained tree which

[1] At Sae Pedro, a thousand miles from the nearest town on the Amazon, Manaos.

[2] See p. 110, *Conquests of the Cross*, Cassell & Co.

S. AMERICAN INDIAN GIRLS.

splits easily, they raise one or two wigwams with pliable boughs and roofs of palm-leaf mats. A few long poles sunk deep into the bed of the lake secures firm anchorage, and here, surrounded by his few worldly goods, the Pamary dwells, living chiefly on fish, and less annoyed than dwellers on land by the mosquitos and other insects, which do not seem to care to come far from the thickly-wooded shore."

Hunting through the forests, building palm-leaf villages, or dwelling in these floating homes on their calm tropic lakes, these simple people seemed to the missionary explorers like little children waiting to be led to the FATHER in heaven.

" I have seen the wild red man in his native solitudes," wrote Mr. Clough, " and found him oftentimes so low in point of knowledge, though not lacking latent intelligence, that he was nothing more nor less than a giant baby. I have found him a stolid, though earnest listener, and believe the Gospel would be to him what it is to all who believe it—the power of GOD unto salvation."

The great dark sphere was open, with its waiting multitudes, and for ten years the S. American Missionary Society worked with encouraging results. A strong and durable mission house was built in the heart of the forest, a school was gathered round it, and helpful work begun. But in 1882 the Society came to the conclusion that "the lack of men fitted for the peculiar work, the trying climate of the Amazon, the great distance from the sea, and from any civilized centre, and above all, the difficulty of supervision by the Bishop, appeared to render the working of the mission impracticable."

And so the nascent effort was relinquished. The simple forest children were left to live and die " having no hope, and without GOD in the world." And for all the thousands of the Upper Amazon can tell, in this year of grace 1894, JESUS has never come to save His people from their sins. "The neat mission house stands out there in the forest, a mournful memento of an abandoned mission field."

*     *     *     *     *

Outside the Fuegian, Paraguayan, and Chili missions, no work for CHRIST is to-day being done among S. America's 5,000,000 aborigines. One Gospel has been translated into the Quichua language, which 3,000,000 of them speak. But no one is teaching them to read it, no one illustrating its good news by lip and life. Into the Guarani, spoken by the unreached Indians of Paraguay, only the Sermon on the Mount has been translated.

Could they but read, those heathen might ponder the strange words : " Ye are the salt of the earth. . . Ye are the light of the world. Let your light shine."

What a reproach to the churches of to-day lies in those words of JESUS there, uncomprehended, in those heathen hands! What a pathetic plea is the darkness of these millions, that the charge those words contain should be fulfilled !

" Ye are the light " who read these words. " Let your light *shine!* "

Just across the ocean thronging conferences of Christians are sitting at spiritual feasts, hanging on the lips of popular divines, and pronouncing on themselves the benedictions of the beatitudes.

Could they but read, those heathen hearts might wonder at that Sermon on the Mount, with its commandment, " Seek ye first the Kingdom of GOD."

How can they seek that Kingdom of which they have never heard ? —but if *these* sought it first. . .

&ast; &ast; &ast; &ast; &ast;

Until when are they to be thus abandoned ?

The words of the isolated Araucanian worker recur, as expressing their unheard appeal : " *How long am I to be left here alone ?* "

" How long ? "

It seems the utterance of these neglected millions ; the utterance, too, of the great heart of CHRIST, who stands in spiritual presence among them as He stands among us,—sorrowing for their darkness, longing for their uplifting, yearning for some human heart through which His words may reach them—and who stands there alone.

## CHAPTER VIII.—CONCLUSION.

### "I WILL SEEK THAT WHICH WAS LOST."

> "I will seek that which was lost, and bring again that which was driven away, and will bind up that which was broken, and will strengthen that which was sick. . . . I MYSELF will feed My sheep, and will cause them to lie down, saith the LORD. . . . They shall be no more consumed with hunger."—EZEK. xxxiv. 16, 15.
>
> "I will give you shepherds according to Mine own heart, which shall feed you with knowledge and understanding."—JER. iii. 15.
>
> "I do send thee unto them."—EZEK. ii. 4.

WE were sitting in the study at Harley House, drawing up the monthly prayer-roll of our Missionary Union. We had come to South America.

"Three days are by far too much to give South America," proclaimed the general verdict.

"Remember how large it is," ventured a special pleader.

"Hardly any population," replied the chairman of committee.

"Thirty-seven millions seem a good many? Besides, how dark they are !"

"Well, we might give them one day ; the need is very great," the general verdict granted.

"But it is so large ! Why not one day for the northern States and the Guianas, one day for the four great republics of the west, and one for the south and Brazil ?"

"*No* one will understand these names," was the emphatic answer. "'*Venezuela*'! But where is Venezuela ? And '*Bolivia*'! Who knows anything about it ? '*English Guiana, French Guiana, Dutch Guiana*'! You will frighten folk away."

So the resolution passed. South America was cut down to one day, its lands and needs included in the abbreviation " Brazil, etc."

The scene was typical. It was the modern missionary world in miniature. Half a century ago Allen Gardiner wrote with a heavy heart: " While efforts to spread Christianity in other parts of the world are carried on with vigour, all animation dies when South America is but hinted at. Collective voices seem to say with a soft murmur, ' It is the natural inheritance of Pope and pagan—let it alone.' "

To-day the " soft murmur of collective voices " seems to pronounce the same opinion.

The newly-published Free Church world-map of foreign missions entirely omits the Western Hemisphere. The Church Missionary Society's crest reads, definitely, " Founded 1799 for Africa and the East." The new *Missionary Encyclopedia* contains no heading " South America," and no article on the continent as a whole, though valuable information is given under special countries, such as " Brazil, etc." The recently published Baptist centennial survey of heathendom and the *Baptist Handbook*, like Mr. Robert Young's *Modern Missions*, and Mr. F. W. Brigg's *Missions Apostolic and Modern*, do not refer to the subject.[1] In Dr. George Smith's *Short History of Missions*, two or three brief allusions to parts of South America exist, but no attempt at the complete and valuable view given of other spheres.

Glance at last year's reports of the entire missionary effort of the Presbyterian, Baptist, and Wesleyan churches of this country. From cover to cover you will find no allusion to the needs of South America. Did none of these churches through 1893 give it a single thought? The C.M.S. *Intelligencer* for the same period, and *The Missionary World*, by Mr. Eugene Stock, contain single paragraphs mentioning Patagonia, but no more.

[1] Mr. Young, we believe, purposes to refer to South America in a later edition of his book, should this be called for. The *Baptist Handbook* prints in an appendix a few lines statistical summary of American work in Brazil.

*Foreign Missions, their Relations and Claims*, by Dr. R. Anderson, contains one brief reference to the subject. *Problems of Religious Progress*, by Dr. Dorchester, like Dr. Pierson's *Divine Enterprise of Missions*, mentions the discovery of South America, but goes no further. Mr. A. Thompson, in his *Foreign Missions*, speaks of the New World as a sphere of labour, but makes no attempt to plead its claims.

One turns from the pages of these missionary books, inclined to ask " Does South America exist at all?  Has it no place in the missionary world, no relation to the progress of humanity ? "

We do not blame these writers, nor the scores of others whose similar omissions might be cited.  We do not blame the Societies that have left the charge of this vast land, as far as our country is concerned, to a single Church agency,[1] which has but twenty-five missionaries all told, reaching only the small English-speaking populations of a dozen districts, besides three Indian centres.  Other needs in other lands claim the attention of the churches, and no organization can be expected to embrace the whole world.  But, facing the thirty-seven millions of South America, we can but ask, *Should not these too be reached?*

It was probably natural that amid the urgent claims of heathendom, newly opened to evangelistic effort, our century of missions should have overlooked this sphere.  Absorbed by the needs of Africa, India, China, and other pagan lands, we have thought of South America as at least nominally Christian, and have said, " Let us go first to the most needy."  But this has been a mistake, arising in great part from ignorance.  Increasing acquaintance with this continent has taught us that its people are as needy as any in heathendom.  True, they have Roman Catholicism ; monks in grey and black

---

[1] The South American Missionary Society, which has clergy or laymen in Patagones, Rosario, Chupat, Buenos Ayres, Salta and Fray Bentos, Rio de Janeiro, Pernambuco, São Paulo, Lota, Chanaral, and Araucania ; and missions at Keppel Island, Tekenika, and Ooshooia, Fuegia, and in the Paraguayan Chaco ; besides granting £100 a year to a mission in Panama.  Offices, 1, Clifford's Inn, Fleet Street, London, E.C.

and brown walk the streets of their cities, and crosses and churches abound ; but, as a recent writer says, the religion preached and practised is " only idolatry cloaked—and very little cloaked—under a few Christian names and phrases."

" Rome does hold up CHRIST ? Yes, but what CHRIST does Rome hold up? A helpless infant in a mother's arms, a helpless man hanging dead upon a Cross, a wafer in a priest's hand. An unattainable CHRIST, except as brought by priest and mother : not a living, risen, present SAVIOUR of men."

Test this religion by its fruits. Does it set free from sin ? Only the pure in heart see GOD, and whatever Romanism has done for the 37,000,000 of South America it has not made them *this*. How can it, since it keeps from them the truth which sanctifies ?

" Very few persons here can read at all," writes a Brazilian worker. " And many of those who can are afraid to buy a Bible, lest they should be excommunicated, or meet with some great calamity. . . . They never hear a word in explanation of the Scriptures. During the five years I have been in Brazil I have never heard of a Romish priest reading the Word of GOD to his congregation."

" When we are asked," writes Mr. Milne, " the reason for the existing difference between Anglo-Saxon and Latin America, our explanation is, that it is not, as most are ready to affirm, a matter of race, but one of principle. With the Bible in their hands, and because of the Bible, the English immigrants passed over to America to found the most powerful States of the world. In these States we have the pledge and proof of what Latin America might and would have been, had the foundation been laid the same. . . .

" The calcined ashes and half-burnt masses of hair of her noblest sons, who, with the Bible in their hands, and because of the Bible, laid down their lives at the stake on the Quemadero de la Cruz, testify that Spain herself could have supplied the men. Had *they* been allowed to escape and lay the foundation of South America, instead of hordes of adventurers with insatiable thirst for gold and rapine, how vastly different would have been its condition to-day !

" What has South America not lost ? "

But the Book is not lost ! We hold it in our hands. And its power for South America is the same as for us.

"Often,' writes Sr. Penzotti from Peru, "when weary with the work of the day, canvassing the mining districts or saltpetre works with a bundle of Bibles, and holding services at night, my heart has been rejoiced in the midst of the fatigue to see that GOD so prospered the work. . . . . At Taltal I met a man who had been truly converted by a simple reading of a New Testament dug from the ruins of a house which had been destroyed by a tidal wave."

Do we not owe this Book to South America ? Millions there can read, and have but little literature to satisfy their newly-wakened craving for mental food. Should we not circulate the Scriptures [1] among them far and wide ?

Few lands challenge Christendom to-day with such imperative appeal as this neglected continent. Is there no meaning in the fact that He who has commanded us to "preach the Gospel to every creature," has during our own day thrown down the papal domination that closed South America to missions a few years back ? We watch His hand in providence opening heathen countries, and we rise with joyful confidence to obey the great commission, as one by one India, Japan, China, Central Africa, and even hermit Korea and Thibet, are for the first time in the history of the world placed within our reach. Shall we not recognise the same Hand doing the same work here ? Shall we not rise from ages of neglect to exercise the same love, prayers, and labour for this land as for those ? Who overthrew the Popish rule of Spain in Paraguay in 1811, in Venezuela and Ecuador in 1830, in Colombia in 1819, in Chili a year before and Peru three years later ; in the Argentine in 1853, Uruguay 1825, and Bolivia in 1880 ? Who overturned the papal *régime* of Portugal in Brazil in 1822 ? Who led to the proclamation of religious liberty at the same dates in eight out of these ten republics, and

---

[1] " Men should be sustained for this special work. Millions of tracts adapted to the people's need might well be circulated. Translations of tracts written for people familiar with the Bible, and living in Protestant countries (and this includes nearly all tracts written originally in English), are not suitable. Special literature is needed for these lands. For direct circulation of the Bible few cheap editions are so attractive as the illustrated portions of the Gospel, published by Mr. Walters, St. Paul's Churchyard, London.'—C. H. Bright, Pegu.

to the recent disestablishment of Romanism in Brazil? Is there no purpose behind the providence that has hidden some of the richest mineral wealth of the world in these republics, and is opening them up, in our own day, by over 50,000 miles of telegraph lines, and by railways that extend in Brazil already 6,657 miles, in the Argentine 8,023 miles, and 1,127 miles in Peru alone? [1]

THE CHAUPICHACA BRIDGE ON THE OROYA RAILWAY, PERU. ANDES SCENERY.

The treaty of 1861, between the latter country and Brazil, arranged that full liberty of communication should be granted through the whole course of the Amazon; steamers now ply regularly between the

---

[1] "The Government railway system of Peru, opened within the last twenty years, is among the wonders of the New World. Peru now owns, for its area, a greater mileage of railway than any other of the American States.

"The costly Oroya line, with its coast terminus at Callao, laid over both ranges of the Cordilleras, with its stupendous gradients and zig-zag windings up the mountain slopes, is assuredly one of the grandest engineering undertakings in the world. Another line in the south, connecting the port of Mollendo, *via* Arequipa, with Puno on Lake Titicaca, is also a great engineering work. It is 346 miles in length. . . . Steep cuttings, superb viaducts, and reverse tangents, up rough and steep slopes to heights of 14,600 feet above sea level are among the features of this bold undertaking, which brings the temperate regions of Titicaca and the Bolivian cities beyond, within easy reach of the Pacific Ocean.

"These railways (which in 1879 comprised twenty-two lines, representing an outlay of £35,994,920), though at first costing such a ruinous sum, that it is doubtful if the Government will ever be financially repaid for their construction, will prove of the highest utility in the evangelisation of the country." (*See Student's* and *Chamber's Encyclopedia,* and *The Engineer.*)

Atlantic and the base of the Andes (within 220 miles of Callao, on the Pacific), thus giving access to the eastern half of the three great republics of Ecuador, Bolivia, and Peru. The heart of the continent, and its remotest regions, are to-day within reach and freely open.

Possibly a few years back we might have been excused for leaving South America unreached: the continent was closed to Christian effort. To-day a change has come, that calls for change in us. Are we prepared to meet the summons of the hour?

We owe these long-forgotten souls the tidings of the Gospel. Our LORD commands that His Word be given " to every creature " here. GOD's love warrants it. CHRIST's death demands it. The HOLY SPIRIT is here to enable us for it. A lost world pleads for it. And we, by our own redemption, are debtors to obey.

   *   *   *   *   *

As these pages go to press, the glory of Easter sunshine floods the cities, towns, and hamlets of our island home. Millions are rejoicing in its radiance, young and old, learned and unlettered, upright and erring alike. And among them tens of thousands, conscious of Easter's meaning, Easter's resurrection power, rejoice yet more in the LORD of Easter Day, of whose glory this outward sunshine, even with all its splendour, is but a faint and fleeting symbol. Thousands are echoing the song of the first Easter—" *The Lord is risen indeed!* "—realizing the joy, the deliverance and salvation that His resurrection has brought.

In the south-western world beyond the blue Atlantic, Easter sunshine falls more brightly than in our island home. But how few there know the thrilling strength and gladness of the first Easter greeting,—how few have caught even an echo of the tidings, " The LORD is *risen indeed!* " While our land rings with hallelujahs from souls set free from sin, thirty-seven million men and women in S. America stand sin-bound in the shadow that covered

Calvary. For them it is still "the sixth hour." Gloom of the wrath of GOD against transgression still darkens all their earth. No news has ever reached them that in that Calvary shadow the sins of the whole world were lost. If their eyes seek the SAVIOUR, they either seek in vain, or see dimly a dead CHRIST in the darkness. And in their last extremity appealing—helpless, ruined—"*Lord, remember me!*" the only answer that meets them is the prospect of the leaping lash of Purgatory's fierce fires and lingering pain. The pitiful and tender "*with Me in Paradise,*" is for them still unuttered. And JESUS' "*It is finished*"—the final triumph-peal of an achieved Redemption—is as if it had not been.

Yet over South America GOD breathes an Easter blessing. For South America's salvation JESUS rose. He will yet fulfil His promise—"*I will seek that which was lost, and bring again that which was driven away, and will bind up that which was broken, and strengthen that which was sick. . . . I Myself will feed My sheep, and will cause them to lie down . they shall no more be consumed with hunger.*"

> "CHRIST is risen! He is risen!
> He hath left the rocky prison,
> And the white-robed angels glimmer mid the cerements of His grave;
> He hath smitten with His thunder
> Every gate of brass asunder,
> He hath burst the iron fetters irresistible to save."

But how? How does He do it?

Through human hearts and hands.

'When the disciples parting from Him, looked up to ask, LORD, wilt Thou at this time restore the Kingdom? Wilt Thou complete Thy triumph and subdue Thy enemies? He for reply looked down, and laid the work on them and their successors to all time. "Ye shall receive power ye shall be My witnesses unto the uttermost parts of the earth."

Still, in view of the whole world's need, does He repeat that sentence. Still does He lay on us that charge.

" LORD, wilt THOU save the world ? Wilt Thou assert Thine authority and bring the nations to Thyself ? "

What is the answer—the answer for all the ages ?

JESUS bent over them and said, " YE."

\*      \*      \*      \*      \*

For when 2,500 years ago He promised to " seek that which was lost," He meant that He would seek them through us,—meant that His SPIRIT should move us to help them.

Has He yet helped South America through you ?

You who have money that belongs to Him, why have you not devoted it to South America ? You who are young and free for missionary work, why not give your life to this Neglected Continent ? Are you teaching ? Why not teach there, supporting yourself and evangelising at the same time (see p. 179), as others have done ? You who are working for the SAVIOUR here— secretaries and helpers in Y.M.C.A. and Y.W.C.A., or Christian Endeavour centres—why not seek to serve Him in this wider and so much more needy sphere ? Are you a housekeeper, a governess, a servant, a nurse, without much opportunity of forwarding missions ? Why not carry out your calling in some missionary household in South America, helping, by filling your own post, and using opportunities to reach those who have never heard of CHRIST ?

Ministers here at home,—should not some of you be preachers and evangelists to thousands in these unenlightened lands ? Have you a commission from GOD to preach the Gospel ? In His Name, why not take it to those who know it not ?

You are called an " Independent " ? Why depend on this small home flock, when so large a flock there might depend on you ? Is it not a shame to the Independent Churches of the world, that to South America's 37,000,000 they have only sent one man?   Might not you be the second to go?

You are an Episcopalian?   What unclaimed bishoprics are waiting in the Guianas and the great republics,—Bolivia, Peru, Ecuador, Colombia, and Venezuela, with their twelve to thirteen million souls, and not a single clergyman or Episcopalian Church.

In the Great Day before us, will not these millions rise and ask why we left them as sheep unshepherded?   When will the cry of these lands be heard?   When the voice of JESUS that urges you to go?

Why work here among a handful, whom others would be reaching if you were far away, when you might help these multitudes whom no one cares to bless?

Home needs are great?   Is that so?   Here, where everybody labours, where every one can know GOD, if they will?   Home needs are great here where we have one ordained minister and scores of Christian workers to every eight hundred of our population?

Yes, they are very great here.   Think, then, *what must they be* where no one has preached CHRIST?

Like Lazarus laid in his sores and suffering at the rich man's door, South America in its spiritual need is laid at our threshold.

What are you going to do for it?

You have read these pages?   Never again can you say you did not know.

By the value of souls, the shortness of time, the greatness of the field before us, *do something definite for South America.*

Practical help is needed; help such as Carey gave to India, Livingstone to Africa, Hudson Taylor to Inland China.   Where is South America's modern missionary apostle?

You cannot go?   Then give.   Collect.   Interest friends.   Circulate this

book.   Tell the young folks and others about these long-forgotten lands.
Study them.   Pray for them.   Work for them.   Means will be forthcoming.
Ways will be opened to you as you seek them from the LORD.

   *   *   *   *   *

 Are we seeking fulness of spiritual blessing, the HOLY GHOST in us
in mighty power?   We can only claim that gift as we fulfil its conditions.
Self-centred lives, hearts contentedly neglectful of the perishing, *cannot* be
fully blessed.   For the SPIRIT OF GOD can only dwell with those who are
GOD-like, who share His love, His self-sacrifice for all.   And only when
obedient can we really claim the gift :—

  "THE HOLY GHOST, WHOM GOD HATH GIVEN TO THEM THAT
       OBEY HIM."

 **J Purpose** by the help of **God** to give

to His

Service in South America, to pray

especially for

and to seek to make

The needs of

known, felt, and met by other Christians.

Signed

Address

Date

Communications from friends volunteering for service or desirous of assisting by gift or in any other way in Mission work in South America, may be sent to

## IN ENGLAND.

Mr. JACKSON,
Missionary Training Home,
10, Drayton Park, London, N.

H. MAXWELL WRIGHT, Esq.
c/o Messrs. Marlborough & Co.,
51, Old Bailey, London, E.C.

Dr. GRATTAN GUINNESS,
The East London Institute for Home
and Foreign Missions,
Harley House, Bow, London, E.

## IN AUSTRALASIA.

Dr. and Mrs. WARREN,
Training Home, Exeter,
South Melbourne, Victoria.

## APPENDIX.

## Help for Brazil.

PASTOR JAMES FANSTONE, OF PERNAMBUCO.

WE shall rejoice if readers of this book will put themselves in communication with the Association "HELP FOR BRAZIL," which, formed in 1892, has for its object to assist the Brazilian Churches founded in 1855 by Dr. Kalley, whose portrait appears on page 53 of this book. Although self-supporting, these Churches are chiefly composed of poor members who are unable to meet the whole of the needs attendant on the opportunities and developments of their own evangelistic work, and who are greatly in need of teachers for the many outlying stations.

The Association, extracts from whose prospectus we subjoin, promotes the evangelisation of Brazil from various centres, especially from Rio and Pernambuco. Further information will be gladly given by the Secretary,—Mrs. R. R. Kalley, Campo Verde, Tipperlinn Road, Edinburgh.

## "HELP FOR BRAZIL."

*Hon. Treasurer.*—DENHOLM YOUNG, Esq., 52, Braid Road, Edinburgh.
*Hon. Secretary.*—Mrs. R. R. KALLEY, Campo Verde, Tipperlinn Road, Edinburgh.
*Hon. Medical Examiner of Scottish Applicants.*—JOSEPH BELL, Esq., M.D., F.R.C.S.
*Bankers.*—THE BANK OF SCOTLAND.
*Representative and Superintendent in Brazil.*—Pastor JAMES FANSTONE, Post Office,
Pernambuco, Brazil ; or Campo Verde, Tipperlinn Road, Edinburgh.

*Council.*—Rev. WALTER BROWN, 78, Craiglea Drive, Edinburgh ; Rev. W. H. GOOLD,
D.D., 28, Mansionhouse Road, Edinburgh ; H. GRATTAN GUINNESS, M.D., F.R.G.S.,
Harley House, Bow, London ; Mrs. R. R KALLEY, Campo Verde, Tipperlinn Road, Edin-
burgh ; JAMES L. MAXWELL, Esq., M.D., 45, Highbury Park, London ; Mr. and Mrs. W.
HIND SMITH, Exeter Hall, London ; E. DENHOLM YOUNG, Esq., W.S., 52, Braid Road,
Edinburgh.

"He goeth before."—JOHN x. 4.

Prayer, sympathy, men and means are asked, in the name of the LORD JESUS, for
Brazilian Christians, and for the multitudes still lying in unrelieved spiritual darkness.

**ORGANISATION.**—The Council of "HELP FOR BRAZIL" exists in two parts
Executive, in Edinburgh ; Advisory, in London. Various well-known Christians have given
their names as referees.

**BASIS.**—A short exposition of the faith and practice of the Brazilian Churches, generally corresponding to the basis of the Evangelical Alliance. A translation of this from the
original Portuguese can be seen by those desiring it. With this statement, any seeking to
work in connection with " HELP FOR BRAZIL" are required to signify their agreement.

**INFORMATION** respecting work done is furnished from time to time by an
"*Occasional Letter,*" which will be gladly forwarded by the Secretary. *To Brazil by Way
of Madeira* (Tract and Book Society, 99, George Street, Edinburgh) tells the story of the
origin of the work.

MR. JAMES FANSTONE, for fifteen years a missionary in Pernambuco, who long supported himself there by teaching English while carrying on his missionary work, and
whose efforts were instrumental in the formation of this Association, is its recognised representative and superintendent in Brazil. In 1893 he took out one new worker ; this year
(1894) he is taking out four more, who we trust will be soon followed by others. He has
frequently addressed British Christians on needs and openings in Brazil, and is grateful for
all opportunities to do so when in this land.

VOLUNTEERS FOR BRAZIL, and all who are willing to help in the passage, outfit,
and support of workers there, are invited to communicate with Mr. Fanstone, or with
the Secretary of the Mission.

# The South American Mission Staff.

STATISTICAL TABLES,[1] prepared from returns from all societies working in South America, have been printed for this book, giving the number and names of the stations of each society, with the number of missionaries (male and female), native helpers, communicants, and adherents located at each centre. Owing to lack of space, we have been obliged to omit these lists, but have summarised their totals in the subjoined and two following tables. Readers wishing to see the figures in detail can have them for 4d. post free, from Miss Guinness, Harley House, Bow, London, E.

Should a superficial study of the following statistical pages give an impression that much is being done for South America, readers are referred for the other side of the question to the diagrams on pp. 79, 80, and especially on pp. 95, 96.

Thank God, strong work has been attempted and done. The American Churches have 86 men and 113 women, and the English, 104 men and 84 women, in the field to-day. But comparing this force, all told, with the needs of South America, it is *as if we had four men and women to reach an area as large as England and Scotland ; as if to evangelise the 90,000 to 100,000 of Derby or Huddersfield we had only got one man.*

### SUMMARY OF PROTESTANT MISSION WORK IN SOUTH AMERICA.

| Country. | Area. Sq. miles. | Population. | No. of Societies at work. | Total No. of Stations. | Total No. of Missionaries (M. & W.) | No. of Converts. | No. of Non-Christians. | On an average one Missionary to |
|---|---|---|---|---|---|---|---|---|
| Guiana | 201910 | 390000 | 6 | 36 | 110 | 70389 | 319611 | 3545 |
| Paraguay | 98000 | 400000 | 3 | 1 | 5 | 924 | 399076 | 80000 |
| Uruguay | 72110 | 750000 | 3 | 2 | 5 | 2406 | 747594 | 150000 |
| Ecuador | 157000 | 1260000 | — | — | — | — | 1260000 | — |
| Bolivia | 507360 | 1450000 | — | — | — | — | 1450000 | — |
| Venezuela | 593943 | 2200000 | 1 | 1 | 1 | 44 | 2199956 | 2200000 |
| Peru | 463747 | 3000000 | 3 | 2 | 9 | 351 | 2999649 | 333333 |
| Chili | 293970 | 3300000 | 5 | 14 | 61 | 2391 | 3297609 | 54098 |
| Argentine | 1125086 | 4000000 | 6 | 14 | 27 | 9612 | 3990388 | 148148 |
| Colombia | 501773 | 4200000 | 2 | 3 | 12 | 161 | 4199839 | 350000 |
| Brazil | 3209878 | 16000000 | 8 | 33 | 116 | 12767 | 15987233 | 137931 |
| | 7287777 | 36050000 | 106 | 346[2] | | 99045 | 36860955 | |

[1] The figures for the areas and population of the South American republics, given in these tables, and throughout the second section of this book, have been taken from Elisée Reclus' newly published *South America (Universal Geography,* Vol. XVIII. Virtue, London). Figures as to railways, etc., are from the *Statesman's Year Book.* Statistics of home Church work have been drawn from *Ha.'ell's Annual,* the *Baptist Handbook, Wesleyan Kalendar,* and from correspondence with Association Secretaries ; while our summary of the mission staff of South America has been compiled from tables sent to all the societies concerned, and filled in by the Secretaries of each mission.

[2] To these must be added the 14 workers in Tierra del Fuego and the Falkland Islands, two travelling agents of the British and Foreign Bible Society, and 13 Salvation Army workers, whom, for want of accurate data from headquarters, we are unable to locate. The Waldensians in Uruguay have two missionaries who do something for the Spanish-speaking people.

# Summary of American Missions in South America.

| Society. | Republic. | No. of Stations | No. of Out-Stations | No. of Male Missionaries | No. of Women Missionaries | No. of Native Helpers and Preachers etc. | No. of Communicants | No. of Adherents | Date of Commencement in South America |
|---|---|---|---|---|---|---|---|---|---|
| Methodist Episcopal Church North. | Argentine Repub. | 3 | 11 | 5 | 7 | 93 | 1411 | 1450 | 1836 |
| | Brazil | - | 3 | | | 8 | 200 | 550 | |
| | Paraguay | | 2 | | | 10 | 114 | 800 | 1867 |
| | Peru | 1 | 1 | 0 | 2 | 22 | 125 | 200 | |
| | Uruguay | 1 | 7 | 1 | 1 | 25 | 481 | 1000 | |
| Methodist Episcopal South | Brazil | 0 | 12 | 10 | 15 | | 933 | 3742 | 1875 |
| American Presbyterian N. & S. | Chili | 4 | 1 | 7 | 6 | 14 | 205 | - | 1861 |
| | Colombia | 3 | - | 5 | 7 | 17 | 414 | - | 1856 |
| | Brazil | 13 | 52 | 20 | 28 | 52 | 3898 | | 1856 |
| Southern Baptist Convention. | Brazil | 4 | 30 | 10 | 11 | 10 | 453 | - | 1879 |
| Bishop Taylor's Mission. | Chili | 6 | - | 14 | 28 | 10 | 250 | 1500 | 1880 |
| American Episcopal. | Brazil | 3 | 4 | 4 | 5 | 0 | 140 | 700 | 1880 |
| American Bible Society. | Venezuela and Central America | 1 | | 1 | | 4 | | | 1888 |
| | Peru, Ecuador, Colombia, Chili, Bolivia | 1 | | 1 | | 0 | | | 1887 |
| | | | | | | (Grants made to the Valparaiso Bible Society) | | | |
| | Paraguay, Argentine, Uruguay | 1 | | 1 | - | 14 | | | 1864 |
| | Brazil | 1 | | 1 | | 16 | | | 1870 |
| Total—7 Societies | 10 Republics. | 44 | 123 | 86 | 113 | 313 | 8513 | 15248 | |
| West Indian Conference. | British Guiana | 6 | - | 10 | | 442 | 3656 | 18800 | 1815 |
| **TOTAL** | | 50 | 123 | 96 | 113 | 755 | 12169 | 34048 | |

# English and Scotch Missions in South America.

| Society. | Country. | No. of Stations. | No. of Out Stations. | No. of Missionaries. | No. of Female Missionaries. | No. of Native Helpers and Preachers. | No. of Communicants. | No. of Adherents. | Date of Commencement in South America. |
|---|---|---|---|---|---|---|---|---|---|
| South American Missionary Society. | Falkland Islands. | 1 | | 3 | 2 | 4 | 6 | Inds. 25 30 | |
| | Tierra del Fuego. | 2 | 5 | 5 | 4 | 11 | 35 | 300 | |
| | Argentine Repub. | 4 | 6 | 6 | 3 | (? Welsh) | 142 | 2805 | |
| | Uruguay . . . | 1 | | 6 | | | 94 | 250 | 1854 |
| | Paraguay . . . | — | 16 | | 4 | 1 | | — | — | |
| | Brazil . . . . | 3 | | 2 | 1 | — | 60 | 300 | |
| | Chili. . . . . | 3 | 5 | 3 | 3 | — | 46 | 570 | |
| | Panama . . . . | 1 | | 2 | | | | ... | |
| Moravian Missionary Society. | Dutch Guiana or Surinam | 17 | 6 | 35 | 35 | 230 | 8307 | 19505 | 1735 |
| | British Guiana (Demerara) | 2 | 19 | 2 | 2 | 22 | 375 | 403 | 1878 |
| London Missionary Society. | B. Guiana . | 1 | | 1 | 1 | 17 | 482 | 1500 | 1821 |
| Society for Propagation of the Gospel. | Guiana . | 8 | 9 | 9 | -- | 30* | 5000* | 10000* | 1861 |
| British and Foreign Bible Society. | Argentine Repub. | 1 | 4 | 1 | | 6 | The British and Foreign Bible Society make an annual grant to the Valparaiso Bible Society. | | |
| | Brazil . . . | 1 | 6 | 1 | | 7 | | | |
| | Chili. . . . | 1 | 4 | | 1 | 5 | | | 1824 |
| | Peru . . . | 1 | | | | | | | |
| | Guiana . . . | 1 | 1 | 2 | | 3 | | | |
| Brethren. | B. Guiana . | 1 | 2 | -- | 6 | 7 | 1500 | — | |
| | Argentine . | 1 | | | 2 | 2 | — | | |
| Dr. Kalley's Churches. | Brazil . | 3 | 8 | 5 | 4 | 20 | 495 | 1115 | 1855 |
| Salvation Army. | Argentine . Uruguay . | 2 | | 14 | 19 | 20 | — | 230 | 1890 |
| Totals—8 Societies. | | 53 | 5? | 101 | 84 | 375 | 16602 | 36063 | |
| Totals from last page | | 50 | 123 | 96 | 113 | 755 | 12169 | 34048 | |
| Grand Total (16 Societies, 12 Countries) | | 103 | 173 | 200 | 197 | 1130 | 28771 | 70111 | |

\* Approximate figure given by the S. P. G.

# THE EAST LONDON INSTITUTE
## For Home and Foreign Missions.

London Centre—HARLEY HOUSE, BOW. E.
Country Branch—HULME CLIFF COLLEGE, CUR BAR, DERBYSHIRE.
Young Women's Branch—DORIC LODGE, BOW, LONDON, E.
Nurses' Training Home—BROMLEY HALL, BROMLEY, E.
Home Mission Headquarters—BERGER HALL, BROMLEY, E.

Hon. General Director—H. GRATTAN GUINNESS, D.D., F.R.A.S.
Hon. London Director—DR. HARRY GUINNESS.
Hon. Secretary—MRS. H. GRATTAN GUINNESS.
Bankers—LONDON AND SOUTH-WESTERN BANK (Bow Branch).

THIS Institute was founded in 1872 under a pressing sense of the claims of the eight hundred millions of heathen who are in this nineteenth century still utterly unevangelized; and of the need of a practical Training Home, where Christian young men and women, of **any evangelical denomination**, gifted for GOD's service and sincerely desirous to devote themselves to it, might be freely received and tested, instructed in the truth, exercised in various branches of evangelistic labour, and, when sufficiently prepared, **helped to go forth as missionaries** to any country or sphere to which GOD might providentially open their way.

The need for, and the benefit of, such an Institute may be judged from the fact that, during the nineteen years that have elapsed since its commencement, **over 3,800** young men and women have applied to be received; that more than **1,200** have been accepted, and that of these about **700** are at the present time labouring in the Gospel, either in the Home or the Foreign field. One hundred and twenty are at present studying in the Institute, and passing out, at the rate of one every week on an average, into missionary spheres.

~~~~~~~~~~

# THE CONGO BALOLO MISSION.

*Headquarters at Harley House, Bow, E.; Hon. Sec., Dr. HARRY GRATTAN GUINNESS.*

### Founded 1888, for the Evangelization of
## THE BALOLO NATION OF THE UPPER CONGO.

### The Mission is Evangelical and Undenominational, has already sent out 42 Workers to LOLO LAND.

Both the Institute and the Congo Balolo Mission are dependent on the free-will offerings of the LORD's people. They are carried on in faith in Him, backed by no Church or denomination, but receiving gratefully help from all who care for the heathen and desire the spread of the Gospel of CHRIST. Their needs are large and constant. The expenditure on all accounts is from £20,000 per annum, and contributions are received with thanksgiving to GOD. Donors' names are not published, but numbered on the lists of donations published monthly in REGIONS BEYOND, the organ of the Institute, of the Congo Balolo Mission, and of the Regions Beyond Helpers' Union. A duly audited balance-sheet appears annually.